# Cecil's Story

Christina Lynne

# Copyright

## Content Note

*This book is a work of fiction. Characters, places, and incidents are either products of the author's imagination or are used fictitiously. Any resemblance to actual events, locales, or persons, living or dead, is entirely coincidental.*

*This novel includes references to domestic violence, non-graphic physical violence, and a non-graphic depiction of murder/suicide. These elements are part of the story's exploration of trauma, family legacy, and the consequences of violence.*

*Readers who may find these topics distressing are encouraged to proceed with care.*

# Dedication

*Dedication*

This book is dedicated to the readers who helped make 13 Miles North *such a success—and who asked for more.* Cecil's Story *was written at the request of readers who wanted to understand what shaped Cecil and what made him a villain. Your curiosity, enthusiasm, and continued support made this book possible. Thank you for coming back for more—enjoy.*

*Acknowledgments*

*I am deeply grateful to my family and friends, especially my spouse and parents, for their constant encouragement and belief in me. Thank you, Mom, Dad, Matt, and my many supportive friends who showed up to book sales and signing events to cheer me on—your presence meant more than you know.*

*Kristine, thank you for being my Emotional Support Human, for pushing me past my fear of speaking, and for standing beside me at so many events. I couldn't have done this without you.*

*Special thanks to Belinda and the Good Vibe Tribe for hosting my very first author event and for reminding me to keep going. Thank you for helping me turn my "mess into a message."*

*And to Dixie—thank you for your mentorship, your friendship, and your guidance throughout my author journey. Your support has been invaluable.*

# Part 1: Cedric

An old man sits down beside me as I sit stew in my own misery, bidding me a quick hello. He seems curious about me. Having nothing but time, and being simply bored, I launch into my tale, warning hm that it is a tale which needs to be told in several pieces for full understanding..

Let me draw you in with my story. Sit down with me—you might just find it fascinating. To understand me, you must first know my grandparents, my aunt, my uncles, and my parents. Their experiences shaped me into the man you know—Cecil Amos.

What I am about to tell you is my own story, shaped by all the people in my life. I share it as truthfully as I remember. When I was born, my father, Cedric Amos, was already a successful business owner. However, that is not how his life began.I have no recollection of my grandparents, as they had passed away before I was born. The first time I saw pictures of my grandparents or was told much about them was during a visit to my uncle's farm.

I remember sitting on the fur rug, warming my hands near a crackling fire in the fireplace at my uncle's cozy home on a cold winter evening. As a young man, I listened intently as moments like this didn't happen often. My uncle leaned back in his wooden rocking chair and smiled as he described my grandparents. He had carefully placed a tattered picture in my hand. "Cecil, your grandfather was a German immigrant," he began in a faraway voice. He stroked his chin thoughtfully. He continued, "He was raised on a barley farm. Working the land was all he ever knew. After hearing about America, he decided at a young age that he wanted to try his luck at making his dream a reality." My uncle paused, and I leaned closer, interested in my roots and pondering my own dreams.

My uncle reached into an old wooden trunk with metal strapping sitting near the fireplace. He dug for a moment, and then brought out a yellowed slip of paper. I took it, awed at seeing that it was the deed to the original Amos Homestead. He continued, "Upon arrival in the United States, near what's now Boston, your grandfather was offered land to settle if he stayed. He gladly accepted. Most other settlers were Irish at that time because of the Great Famine. As a German, he felt a bit out of place, but he put practicality ahead of where he may have felt he fit." His face grew stoic as he continued our family's history.

"He put his experience raising crops in his homeland to work and began to farm his newly acquired property. He built himself a small shelter using what he had available." My uncle had another yellowed photograph in his hand that he had been hanging on to as he had spoken. He handed me the next picture, which showed the same young man, now standing proudly near a small shack. Another brief pause as I took in the scene in the picture. "It wasn't much, but a man didn't need much to make himself happy back then. He had a roof over his head and food enough to fill his stomach. These essentials were all he needed."

I was completely enthralled in the tale between the photographs, and my uncle's nostalgic telling of the events that shaped our family. I wanted to take the unique opportunity to learn as much as I could. I propped myself up on my elbows, face cradled in hands, and listened with intensity. When he paused, I interjected insisting that he complete the tale. "Then what, Uncle Curtis?" My eyes were wide with anticipation.

He laughed, amused at my enthusiasm and gladly continued. "After establishing his home and a living, he had another goal. He wanted to find himself a wife. Then his 'American Dream' would be complete." My uncle looked at me with a grin, and I grinned back.

My uncle took a swig of the tea from his tin mug and cleared his throat before continuing. "Now comes the fun part. It wasn't long until he met his future wife, my mama, and your grandmother. She was also from Germany, a descendant of Romani Heritage. He always said he was immediately attracted to her exotic beauty and mysticism. They were young and attracted to each other. There was no reason to wait. Both knew what they wanted, so they married quickly. From everything I have been told and everything I ever saw, they were a happy, loving couple who enjoyed the simple life on their farm. Your papa was born nine months after their wedding. The other three of us came one after another."

I watched as the grin dropped from his face. I wondered what the reason was. Could there be something bad coming in a tale that had been so wonderful so far? My uncle's tone changed, becoming much more serious as if the memory weighed heavily on him. "As we grew older, it was clear that each of us had a very different personality. We were all born and raised on the farm, and each was given responsibility. The two younger boys and I enjoyed the hard work. Your father, Cedric, didn't." He scowled at the end of the sentence and looked directly at me.

My uncle stood, hands crossed behind his back and begun pacing in front of the fireplace as he continued. "Cedric's gift was being very smart. He liked school. He had a sharp memory and a knack for organization. Papa noticed that he had a mind for numbers. His English and handwriting were clearer than the rest of us. He was still just a boy when he was sent to town with a list of what was needed and money. Soon, he was the one in charge of keeping us stocked with supplies and making sure we had enough feed for the animals.

He stopped in front of the bookshelf on the far side or the room, grabbing a book as if to emphasize this part of the story. He continued to talk while leafing mindlessly through the pages. "With time, he was also put in charge of selling goods from the farm. He learned when to expect sale prices to be the highest for the crops and cattle, what crops to grow in the fields, and what brings the highest profit for the family." He stopped, looking at the ceiling and exhaling a deep sigh. "That's how your papa got started in business."

He closed the book, placing it back on the shelf. I noted that he still held something in one of his large weathered hands. He crossed the room and bent down in front of me, carefully handing over the final picture. By now, I knew that no further encouragement was needed for him to finish the story. I took it into my hands and examined it. This picture was of the entire family together: Grandmother, Grandfather, my father, his two brothers, and his sister all stood in front of a small shack. I looked at it and then back at my uncle, trying to identify the people I knew now with the people then. With that, he ended his tale. It is a wonderful memory of a very rare moment where some of what shaped me was disclosed to me. That part of the story would affect me more than my young self could have ever known.

Now, back to the part of the tale that leads you to me, and why I ended up here speaking with you now. I know the rest of the story by heart. My father told me many times, always with pride but also a trace of bitterness. He hoped I would admire him for leaving me a business instead of a farm. Looking back, I sense the emotional burdens that weighed on him. I can also place where my own woes begun. Part of me can't help but pity him for what he lost along the way.

The place is my childhood home on the East Coast. The time is the early 1900s. I clearly remember it was an evening after dinner. We sat out on our porch to enjoy the cool, shaded breeze. My father sat in his favorite rocking chair. My mother was nearby, and I took a seat on the swing.

As I had begun to expect by this time, my father started the familiar tale of how we had gone from poor farm folk to the Elite in the area. His chest puffed out a bit and his words came through a prideful smile. "Son, by the time I was in my teens, our family was no longer poor. Due to the exceptionally gifted young man that I was, we had become one of the most prestigious farming families in the area." He held his chin high as he adjusted his tie.

"I loved caring for the family business, but despised the physical and disgusting side of farm work. Most of all, I hated being forced out of school at an early age just so I could keep up with my growing responsibilities. I longed for a better life." As he spoke, he looked down and his carefully manicured hands as if to ensure none of the dirt from the fields remained on them anywhere. "Although I was proud of myself, I worked twice as hard as my siblings. My two brothers and sister were younger, weaker, and less responsible than I was. Thus, more pressure was on me to get things done. Our family's success weighed heavily on my shoulders. I felt that my abilities were being taken advantage of. I had never felt the connection with family that others talk about. I was far too mature for my age and could not fight the constant feeling that I was different, better than the rest." Now he looked at me and scowled. His arrogance was unmistakable in the way he spoke, but behind those words, I sometimes sensed pain and longing—a need to be understood that he rarely confessed.

As if to drive home the point, he raised his voice. "Son, are you listening to me?"

I jumped a bit at the sharp reprimand. In truth, I had gotten bored and my mind was wandering. I could not let him know that, or I would be facing his wrath. I quickly met his eyes and smiled, feigning interest in the story I had heard many times before. "Of course I am, father."

He cleared his throat, seemingly satisfied that he had my full attention. He began again from where he had left off. "Although our family farm was thriving, I could feel myself slowly wilting in the environment, which failed to challenge me. I did my best to hide how unhappy I was. Of course, I was respectful to the rest of my family, though I kept my distance at best. I thirsted for the companionship of those of similar interests. Since being forced to leave school after completing the sixth grade, my only intellectual stimulation was when I went to town to do business. I picked up any reading materials I could find, from newspapers to used books, when I could afford them. City living called to me..." He would repeat each time he told the story of his success.

To my relief, his story ended there. I knew there was more, but was very grateful he had chosen to end there for the night. I looked over at my mother who appeared to have been paying attention to the story as well. She shot me a quick yet imperceptible grin to indicate that she was equally as uninterested as I was. The evening ended shortly after that, and we were able to retreat to bed without further regaling of the past.

# Part 2: The Building of an Empire

Part 2: The Building of an Empire

Though I disliked my father, I believe I understand him a bit better after living my own life. It saddens me to think about what it must have been like for him. My father did not have any friends his own age. His maturity and reputation had spread among the adults he regularly dealt with throughout the community. They became his friends. He was known as 'the young genius.' This became the standard that I was held to as I grew up.

The local business owners in town came to enjoy his visits more each time they dealt with him. He took a particular liking to the owners of the local General Store, the Banker where his father kept the farm account, and several of the farmers and workers at the cattle yard where he sold the family's livestock.

The thing that truly made me realize his values was how he bragged that he was best known for driving a hard bargain. He insisted on always obtaining top dollar for the wares he sold and haggling with vendors until he talked them into lowering the price. Despite his young age, he quickly became respected amongst all with whom he did business. Already, his true love was money.

The story does get happier for my father, at least for a bit that is. My father's fortune turned for the better. You will have to excuse me if I seem a bit unimpressed. I, myself have a very hard time understanding how he found the lifestyle he chose to be one with any happiness. I am just relaying the story to you as it was told to me by the man himself. You will understand why this information is important later in my story.

Once he turned sixteen, he was approached by the bank owner and asked to work part-time. It was an opportunity for him to receive formal training in finance. My father gladly accepted, with the agreement that he would still work on the family farm. He worked night and day, barely resting between keeping the family farm running smoothly and learning the business from the banker. It was not an easy life for him, but instinct told him it would pay off. While his contempt for the farm was not gone, working at the bank did lessen it, as it gave his mind something to do.

Working at the bank and dressing nicely, many girls had started to notice him despite his quiet demeanor. Soon, his desire grew more to leave the farm completely. Doing so would free up time for a social life outside of work for him to begin courting the beautiful girls he encountered. He knew this would not be possible while he continued to run the family farm and work in town.

The wheels of fate had begun to turn. Upon his eighteenth birthday, my father announced to his family that he was leaving. Up to this point, the only people he had shared his plan with were Uncle Curtis and the Banker who had taken him under his wing. Uncle Curtis had only been privy to his plan to drive home the importance of his brother learning everything needed to run the farm.

My father always seemed to be a bit regretful as he continued on to this part of his story. Maybe there was some conscience within the man. As the story went, my grandmother cried, and my grandfather was angry when my father made the announcement. Knowing that my father was now a grown man and had decided to blaze his own path in life, the family reluctantly wished him well. They knew that there was no stopping him. Trying would only cause further friction.

As I see it now, driven would be my best description of the man. My father's reputation continued to grow once he moved into town and began working full-time at the bank. Many of the businessmen had watched him grow up. The store owners knew him especially well from his supply runs, and their respect for him had only grown as he matured from a brilliant young boy into a full-grown businessman.

It may surprise you, however, it amazes me what that man accomplished with only a grade-school education. If nothing else, I respect him for that reason alone. He took the natural gifts given to him and built upon them. Thanks to the money he saved from his paychecks, he was able to buy the General Store when its elderly owners chose to retire and had no one else to turn it over to. The General Store never closed. The only difference was the face behind the counter.

My father no longer worked for the bank. Now he had his own business to tend to. He moved from the room above the bank to the room above the General Store. With one job, he worked harder than ever to build his own legacy.

He discovered that owning his own business was much more challenging than he had expected. The days were long, the nights short, and the time for rest was almost nonexistent. Yet he kept going. As my father's success grew, he became obsessed. Now you will understand why this is the point in the story that I knew and came to loathe.

No matter how well he did, he wanted more. Greed took over, leaving his gratefulness for his new life as a thing of the past. His personality changed. No longer was he the young man eager to leave a good impression on everyone he met. Now, he was Cedric Amos, a businessman out to build an empire.

By day, he dealt with his growing customer base with a friendly smile and a charming demeanor. By evening, he went home alone or with one of many beautiful women in his arms to meet his physical needs. The very thought of this disgusts me.

The idea of courting many of the beautiful women he encountered dwindled to the occasional meal and then to sharing his bed for a night. His reputation as a ladies' man grew, along with his reputation as a businessman.

The businesses he had once visited as a consumer had now become competitors. While he was personable with the other business owners face-to-face, what he did behind their backs became a point of contention that the other shop owners discussed amongst themselves. His business practices were ruthless. He was willing to do whatever it took to succeed.

This lonely lifestyle pulled him even further away from his family. My father's selfishness escalated as he became successful. Though the Amos family farm was nearby, my father rarely saw his family after moving to town.

Several years passed as my father kept busy, intentionally distancing himself from farm life. He did not want to remember the years working miserably under the hot sun, tolerating his family, and constantly feeling like the odd man out. He wanted to build his own life in the city and would have preferred that no one knew he was related to the rest of the Amos family. Even though they were now well-respected farmers in the area, they were still just that, peasant farmers. He didn't want anyone who was not already aware to discover how he grew up. He didn't want the world to see him as an uneducated farmer now that he was building his empire. Greed was consuming him.

Soon, his mother, who used to enjoy coming to town to socialize, was absent when the family visited for supplies. From what he heard, his mother's health was beginning to decline with her age. My father had failed to take notice when visiting the family. He got through each visit without taking much notice of events at the family farm or of the family members. Mostly, he wanted to get back to his business. His heart seemed to have frozen. He could not be bothered by the lot of others, even the one woman who had birthed and raised him.

My father's withdrawal from society and his love for only his business led to the creation of Amos Enterprises. It started with that one General Store in his hometown on the East Coast of the United States. That store gained popularity because of how he ran it.

As the business continued to grow, his personality became increasingly colder. Soon, the thought of his ailing mother was once again pushed from his mind. Years later, many described his personality as being as cold as an East Coast blizzard. Beautiful women coming in and out of the store no longer drew his attention, and those who joined him for a nightcap became few and far between. His callous manner left him a respected businessman with very few friends.

With the earnings from his store, he saved enough money to build upon its success. He moved out of the apartment above the General Store and now lived in a modest home within the city, which in no way indicated his level of success. He lived meagerly, moving all his earnings back into his store.

He compensated for his lack of social life by throwing his energy into his true love, his growing empire. He grew the business to include several more General Stores in varying locations. The once-small business slowly became a large, well-known chain. Amos Enterprises was now a household name.

# Part 3: A Change in the Amos Family

Part 3: A Change in the Amos Family

Forgive me if my voice falters a bit here. This is where most people begin to doubt me when I relay this story. As I tell it, it sounds unbelievable to even me. I will relay it in as much detail as I remember.

One night, after releasing a random woman from his presence, my father lay alone in his bed. For the first time he could remember, he felt lonely. That night, he tossed and turned in the large king-size bed. The room, though well-heated by a fireplace, felt cold. He hugged his down-stuffed comforter close to his body, trying to warm himself.

Then it came. A vision of his mother. Her illness showed as her once plump frame seemed now small and fragile. Loose skin seemed to hang from her bones. Her once-dark hair had gone completely gray and appeared very thin. Her once olive-colored skin seemed very pale. There were dark circles under her eyes. She stood beside his bed, speechless, with a forlorn look upon her drawn face. Then, as soon as it started, it was over. His eyes shot open as he gasped for air. It had only been a dream. The rest of the night, he was unable to fall back asleep. He lay in bed, tossing and turning until the sun rose.

My father rose from his bed, weary and disturbed by the dream. He had a store to run, so he forced himself to wash and dress. He brushed his hair and looked at his reflection in the mirror. He realized he looked equally as unrested as he felt. He grabbed an apple from his pantry and quickly ate it before heading out the door to walk to work. He hoped the short walk from his home to his store would be enough to make him feel more alert.

On that fateful day, he went about his daily routine. Little did he know that he was about to receive the worst news of his young life.

My grandfather rode into town alone. The purpose of this visit was not to purchase supplies but to pass on the news that my grandmother had passed away. The bell above the door to the General Store jingled, startling my still drowsy father. He turned from the shelf he was stocking to see my grandfather standing at the door. It had been a long time since the two men had seen each other, but not long enough for my father not to notice the grief written all over his own father's face.

Grandfather relayed the message slowly and carefully as not to break down while doing so. The news hit my father hard. He had been putting off returning home, but now it was too late. His mother, the only female figure in his life who represented what a loving relationship should look like, was gone. Never again would he see her smile or hear her hearty laugh; never again would he see his mother and father embrace. Now, the previous night's dream made sense.

She had lived long enough to watch both his brothers marry and his sister get engaged. Now, my grandmother would not live to see him in a relationship, let alone get married. All at once, the reality of how lonely his life was hit him.

He could not face attending my grandmother's funeral alone. He quickly masked his emotions, hiding his grief from my grandfather. He took a deep breath, stood up straight, and coldly offered his condolences, sending my grandfather on his way. He did not return home to see my grandmother's body, nor did he attend the funeral. He knew that he was going to face the wrath of his family, but with my grandmother gone, my aunt Sissy, his baby sister, was the only one that he remotely cared about.

As the day ended, he dragged himself home. That night, he decided he was going to turn to alcohol to help him sleep. He locked his door behind him as soon as he entered his home and headed directly to the cupboard that contained the whiskey. No food was consumed that evening. The fine whiskey burnt more with each sip as it slid down his throat. He sat on the large soft chair in front of the fire and was soon asleep.

"Cedric..... Cedddddddricccccc..." came the eerie voice... He didn't move.

There, in front of him, stood his mother in a long white gown. She looked exactly as she had when he had seen her in his dream. "Cedric. What has become of you, my dear sweet boy?" Her lips appeared to remain still as she spoke. He tried to speak. As he did, she raised one bony finger. He soon discovered that he could not move or speak. "Cedric, you stopped visiting. I got sick, and you never visited. Oh, how it broke my heart. You did not go to your brothers' weddings and stopped watching over your baby sister. What has happened to you? Why have you withdrawn from your family? Were we really so terrible?" She appeared to fade in and out as she spoke. Tears now streamed down the ghostly face.

"Mother," he tried to utter, discovering immediately that he was still unable to speak.

Suddenly, her face turned angry, and her eyes seemed to glow. "Silence! You are not the son I raised! You did not even have enough respect to visit me or come to my funeral! The only thing that matters to you is money!"

Sadness and panic overtook him all at once as he attempted to speak again. His hands, no longer paralyzed, rose to his mouth, and he found no lips where his mouth should be. There was no opening at all—only smooth skin. He struggled to move his body but was still unable to do so.

"If money is all that matters to you, I curse you and your lineage to a life with no happiness aside from what money can bring!" Then she was gone.

His eyes shot open as he gasped. He was still sitting in his chair, where he had fallen asleep. His hands went quickly to his lips. To his relief, his mouth was there. He stood up and found he could move. The fire had long since died, and the room was cold. He walked around his home, carefully checking each room. Nothing was disturbed. The door was still locked.

"It was just a dream," he said aloud. "I drank too much whiskey, and it was just a dream." He carefully made his way to bed and tried to fall back asleep.

# Part 4: Enter Rowena

Part 4: Enter Rowena

The following day, as the sun rose, he stayed in bed longer than usual. He thought about the dream, his life, and his prospects. He knew he was a successful businessman, lonely, and that age was catching up with him. He knew that for his empire to survive, he needed an heir.

He immediately started searching for his new prospect by paying close attention to each woman who entered his store. Though many were married or older, some were clearly available and of marriageable age. Some were farmers' daughters, others were ladies of the night, and some were high-class ladies with connections to surrounding businesses. Because of his social status, they all showed interest in him if he so much as flashed them a smile. He had many women to choose from.

That day, while tending his store, he asked the first young lady that he was attracted to if she would join him for dinner that evening. The sudden change in demeanor surprised the beautiful, young brunette. She flashed him a smile and gladly accepted. After all, who could turn down a meal with the area's most eligible, richest man? Especially when that man was as handsome as Cedric.

The eerie dream involving his mother, his mother's death, and any desire to see his family were soon forgotten. Life went back to normal, aside from my father courting a steady stream of women in search of the one who would become his wife and bear his heir.

This behavior continued for another year. My father courted several women for several months apiece. None of them seemed to be people with whom he could see himself spending any further time. The advantage of this was that his people skills improved. He did become a nicer person and even made a few friends during his time in public. He soon discovered that the time away from his business was bothersome but not entirely unpleasant.

Forgive me if I soften a bit as I continue. This is my favorite part of the story. My father always smiled when he told me about his first meeting with my mother. My heart warms to this day when I think about her. From what he described, my father's mindset suddenly changed when a woman with beauty unlike any he had seen before caught his eye.

My father had been outside sweeping the sidewalk in front of his store. Something told him to look up from his task at just the moment when *she* exited the laundry across from his store.

Her long, curly blonde hair, fair skin, rosy cheeks, and sky-blue eyes, framed by long, thick lashes, had caught the attention of many men. She was unusually tall for a woman and lean aside from her ample womanly curves.

She was a spirited young woman at twenty. No man had yet been enough of a challenge for her. My mother, Rowena, came from an affluent family, and her father had been pushing her to find a good man and marry before her childbearing years passed. She would have preferred to attend college and experience life. She had no interest in becoming a wife or having children at such a young age. Like my father, she had courted several young men; however, as a woman, courting multiple men was frowned upon.

As the story goes, both of their perspectives changed when they met. She knew she had finally found her match. He was ten years her senior. His icy blue eyes left her more captivated than she could have possibly imagined. His thick, slicked-back black hair contrasted with his pale skin and blue eyes. He was clean-shaven, with a pronounced dimple in his very prominent chin. He was lean yet broad-shouldered. In her opinion, he was exactly the way a man should be.

As their gazes connected, his eyes seemed to sparkle. His thin lips parted, showing straight white teeth and a stunning smile. This was the first time that the two had met, and attraction drew them together like a magnetic force.

For my mother, time slowed as he strutted across the dusty, narrow road. All other human activity seemed to halt. My father quickly closed the distance between them. He stopped in front of the worn wooden hitching post that bordered the plank sidewalk where she stood. For a moment, they were both silent. "Hello. My name is Cedric Amos," he said in a deep voice as smooth as silk. "What is your name, Miss?"

My mother extended her dainty hand to my father as he bowed. He accepted her hand and gently placed a kiss on her milky-white skin. Her cheeks reddened slightly, a new experience for her. "Pleased to make your acquaintance, Cedric," she replied in a voice she did not recognize as her own. "My name is Rowena."

It was at that moment that my mother realized who she was speaking with. The owner of Amos Enterprises. He was well known in the area, though she had never met him before. Her family had recently moved to the area, and she was beginning to become acquainted with the region's locals. She had heard of this man and his exploits, but this was their first encounter. She could not believe her luck. She smiled shyly at him, awestruck that a man of his notoriety would approach her.

"Miss Rowena, your beauty rivals that of a mountain sunrise on a dewy morning," he said, not letting go of her hand.

Her blush deepened. "I am flattered," was all that she could muster. Again, there was silence as the two gazed into each other's eyes, seemingly forgetting everything else around them.

"Would you do me the honor of joining me for an evening meal?" Finally, he broke the silence.

"I... I... I...." she stuttered, astounded by her luck.

He chuckled, finding her reaction endearing. "I will take that as a yes," he stated confidently. His smile grew. "I will pick you up at six p.m. May I ask the location of your residence?"

My mother gave him directions to her home, which was located several miles outside town. My father kissed her hand once again and then released it. "I look forward to basking in your beauty this evening, Miss Rowena," he said, turning and walking back toward his store.

She stood; hand in the air, looking at where he had just kissed it until after he had disappeared back into his store. She inhaled deeply and then brought herself back to reality. She was standing in front of the laundry, waiting for her clothing to be finished. As reality set in, she thought about what she had just committed to. A date with the most sought-after, eligible bachelor in the area! She hurried home after retrieving her laundry to tell her parents about the fortune that she had found while in town.

My father finished the rest of his workday, thinking about the events he had just experienced. How had he never noticed this beautiful creature before? Was she new to the area? More so, could she be precisely what he had been searching for? The feeling he had when they touched was what he imagined magic felt like.

The day at the store seemed to drag on forever, an unknown feeling for my father. After what seemed an eternity, closing time finally rolled around. He hurried through the final duties of the day, in a hurry to get home, change into something he found to be presentable for his date, and be on his way to pick up the beautiful young lady.

For the first time, he whistled a happy tune as he closed the door to his store and locked it. With a spring in his step, he headed home. Once home, he quickly dressed in his best suit. This was not to be just another meaningless date. He gave himself one more glance in the mirror to ensure he looked his best and then headed out to the stable to hitch his team of black horses to his buggy. He knew he had to be on time to make a good impression. He hopped on the seat of the buggy with a feeling of excitement in his heart. He clicked his tongue and slapped the reins against the back of the team, sending them into a steady trot in the direction of her home.

The horses kept pace as they headed out of town. He made good time and knew that he would arrive just a bit early. As he approached the home, he observed a well-manicured yard and a large white Victorian-style house with black trim surrounded by flower beds. There was a large stable near the rear of the property and a fence surrounding it. Several fine-boned horses grazed within.

He had not expected the home to be any more than rough logs, like many in the area. The grandeur of the house surprised him. He wondered if Rowena lived here alone or with family. What did the owner of this fine property do for a living? He was hopeful he had finally chosen someone who would be a suitable match for him within his standards and the public eye.

# Part 5: Courting and Commitment

Part 5: Courting and Commitment

As he stopped the buggy in front of the large white house, it was not Rowena who came to the door but an older man. He was a mountain of a man, easily towering six inches above my father and much broader. His portly belly made him appear even more intimidating. The look on his face could be described as nothing other than hatred. His scowl grew as my father exited the buggy, hitched the team, and approached the door. His brown eyes appeared almost black as he glared at the younger man from under thick, bushy eyebrows. My father was terrified; however, he was well-schooled in hiding his emotions. "Good evening, Sir. You are Rowena's father, I would presume?" The man did not speak. "I am Cedric Amos. With your permission, I would like to take Rowena to town for a meal." His voice remained calm and steady, and he did not show an sign of the fear that was about to overcome him at the site of the large surly man.

The man stood planted in front of the entrance to the house, arms crossed, and continued to scowl. Rowena then appeared from behind the mountain of a man, smiling shyly. "Good evening, Cedric. This is my father, Alexander. Father, this is Cedric. Please be nice." The man shifted his weight slightly, and his face softened to a smile at the sight of his daughter.

She looked up into the large man's eyes, determined to shift his attention from Cedric to herself. "Daddy, I told you that Cedric was going to pick me up this evening. Do not act as if you are surprised." She dared to roll her eyes at him.

The large man looked between the two as if deciding how to react. Slowly, he extended a large hand with fingers that resembled sausages toward my father. He cautiously extended his much smaller hand in return. My father's hand was all but crushed in Alexander's grasp. He grinned as my father winced, trying not to show any sign of weakness. "Cedric," He said as he pumped my father's hand up and down in a hearty handshake.

My father freed himself from his grip as quickly and politely as possible. "It is a pleasure to meet you, Sir. May I have the honor of your daughter's company this evening?"

The scowl returned to his face. It was clear that he did not approve of the idea. My mother was of age and had her heart set on going with my father. "Father, I will be going with Cedric now. I will see you when we return." As she finished, she went to his waiting buggy.

"Sir," my father nodded, turning and following my mother. At that moment, they knew it was the beginning of a lasting relationship.

The evening meal was enjoyable. To my father's surprise, the conversation flowed easily from business to personal as the two got to know one another. As the meal was finished, He reached across the table and gently placed his hand on my mother's. He shared that, for the first time, he had enjoyed the evening meeting. She admitted feeling the same. The two shared a warm smile. It seemed that they were made for each other. They agreed to see each other again as their schedules allowed.

The buggy ride home was pleasant, with my mother scooting as close to my father as possible on the seat. She leaned her head onto his shoulder, and the two shared a happy, comfortable silence for the remainder of the ride back to her home. The new couple shared their first kiss that evening. My father helped my mother out of his buggy and politely waited as she safely entered her home.

My father returned home, happy for the first time in many years. That night, he slept peacefully without the disturbance of any dreams.

To my mother's delight, after that night, she became the only woman he was courting. He was gentle and sweet. He even began to limit his time running the business and hired an employee to help at the local location.

My father and mother courted for several months. They were frequently seen together in public. She even visited his store during business hours most days. When he was not working, my father was wooing my mother. His original plan to marry for appearance had long since been forgotten. The longer they were together, the deeper their bond became.

My mother always smelled of lavender, even when she had not tried. She loved to sing, cook, and write. Father loved that she was educated. She had been given the opportunity to complete secondary school. Her intelligence was more attractive to him than her physical appearance. She longed to be more than just a housewife. He recognized in her the partner he had been looking for.

The experience of loving someone was new to them, as they had previously only courted for pleasure. Now, the initial magnetic draw had become so much more. The more they learned about each other, the more they learned that they had in common. The softer side of my father began to show. He brought her flowers, lavished her with gifts, and whisked her off to any location she wanted to go. The money he had amassed was becoming a shared fortune. This woman was the one person he had ever met whom he was willing to share it with.

Soon, my mother joined my father at his store full-time. She learned the accounting books and the inner workings of running the Amos Enterprises Empire. My father knew he needed to make this woman his wife.

As the couple courted, my future grandfather softened toward my father. The two began to respect each other and even became friends. He revealed to my father that he had made his fortune by investing a small amount in the railroad, which had grown as it expanded. The family had settled near the city, where the railroad was, and built their little ranch.

Undenounced to my mother, Father had taken the opportunity to speak to Grandfather alone one evening after a family dinner. He had asked for her hand in marriage and had even brought the ring along to show him. Grandfather hesitated, but after getting to know my father and seeing how he treated her, he could not say no. Now, my father had the blessing he needed in order to proceed with what his heart truly wanted.

There was still one subject that my father had yet to broach with my mother: his family and growing up on a farm. He had not yet disclosed anything to her regarding his start in life. All she knew was the successful man he was now.

After learning how well-to-do my mother's family was and where she had acquired her business knowledge, he was now even more reluctant to reveal his origins to her and more so to her parents.

# Part 6: Introduction to the Amos Family

Part 6: Introduction to the Amos Family

My father was beginning to think more seriously about proposing to my mother, and he thought it only fair that she and her family knew everything about him before doing so. They had been courting for six months. He had finally decided to introduce her to his family, revealing his secret that he had not always been a successful businessman.

On a Sunday after the store closed at its usual time at noon, my father drove his buggy to my mother's house. The visit was not planned, and she was surprised to see him. "Cedric, what are you doing here?" she exclaimed at seeing my father's buggy pull into the yard. She had been outside near the barn, grooming the favorite of her horses.

His nerves were threatening to show through his confident smile, however he managed to keep them at bay. He stopped the buggy, and stepped out of it, hitching his team near where she stood. "Hello, Rowena. You look beautiful today," he said to her as he produced a bouquet of daisies from the seat of his buggy.

Her long hair flowed freely in the slight breeze, and her floral dress swayed side to side. My father could not help but admire her. He knew he was making the right decision, but was having difficulty deciding how to proceed. He smiled warmly, making his way to her side, and scooped her up into his arms in a loving embrace.

My mother smiled back but pushed him away. "What is it that is bothering you, Cedric?"

His smile dropped. "How did you know?"

"After being by your side for six months, I have learned to tell exactly when your face and actions are masking something you don't want to say." My mother smiled knowingly at him.

My father reluctantly pulled away from the rejected embrace. His smile had dropped further upon hearing her words. "I would like to take you to meet my family."

She dropped the brush she had been using to groom her horse. It landed on the ground with a thud stirring up dust as it hit. "Your family? You have never said anything about them before." The astonished look on her face spoke volumes.

He looked down at his boots, nervously kicking at the grass. "Rowena, I have not always been the successful man you see before you now. I would like to show you where I came from and let you decide if you are still interested."

Surprised at his remark, she reached for his hand and grasped it with both of her own. "Cedric, I don't understand. I thought you didn't have any family near here."

His face now ashen, he looked directly at her as he spoke as if to ensure she saw the sincerity with which he spoke. "I do. They live west of town. My family's farm is there. I have not spoken to any of them since my mother's death."

My mother was silent for a moment, leaving my father reluctant to go any further. "Cedric, I am having a difficult time surmising why you have not disclosed this before. I have fallen in love with you, not your past nor your family." Her evident disappointment was enough to sway my father's decision.

"My apologies, my love. It has been a long time since I have associated with them. It's been longer since I've allowed myself to think about my past. Let me explain." He went on to relay the story of how he had grown up, what had driven him to leave, and finally, my grandmother's death. What he left out is how he had driven his family away. My mother agreed to meet his father, brothers, and sister.

"There is more that I need to tell you," my father continued as they made the slow trek to the farm. "I started avoiding my family after I moved to town. I did not want them around my business. I did not see my mother before she died, nor attend her funeral. I was not present at my siblings' weddings, nor have I met the man my sister is betrothed to."

All the shame of not being there for years flooded his mind. The happiness he had felt while falling in love with my mother had been masking the guilt of leaving his family behind. Despite his best efforts, a tear slowly escaped his eye as he realized what success had cost him in the long run.

He stopped the buggy and buried his head in his hands, sobbing. All the emotions he had been suppressing flowed from his eyes at once. My mother allowed him to cry until he could cry no more, all the while rubbing his back in small, soothing circles.

Anguish overcame him. He could only imagine what was going through the head of the woman he wanted to spend the rest of his life with. "My love, they will never forgive me. Can you forgive me? Can you see me as anything other than a monster now that you know?" His eyes again welled with tears, threatening to escape as he spoke.

For a moment, neither spoke. Their eyes connected, and the emotions simply flowed between them. Her eyes were now filling with tears of her own. She scooted closer to him on the seat of the buggy, and they joined hands. "My dearest, handsome man, as I have said so many times before, there is nothing you can do to stop me from loving you. I love you more for your honesty. That may have been who you were, but it most certainly is not who you are now."

The young couple met in a passionate embrace. Now, the air was clear between them. There were no more secrets. My father looked around them, noticing the beauty of the rolling hills flourishing with thick green grass waving in the breeze. They had stopped next to a large Cottonwood tree. There was nothing around them other than the rough-cut road, worn into the scenery by many wagons traveling this path over the years. Wildflowers of varying varieties spotted the green scenery near the road. He exited the buggy without warning and moved quickly to the side where my mother sat.

Taken aback by the sudden change in his demeanor, my mother sat frozen in the buggy seat. "What are you doing, Cedric?"

He dropped to one knee in the lush green grass beside the buggy. "Rowena Lenore Essington, would you do me the honor of accepting me as your husband?"

He had not planned to propose until after she had met his family; however, after the emotional conversation, the moment felt right.

It was Rowena's turn to spill tears—tears of joy. "Yes, Cedric! Is there really any other answer I could give other than yes?"

He produced the ring box from his pants pocket and carefully slid the thin gold band adorned with a large, crystal-clear diamond onto her hand. She beamed at him. "Now get up off the ground, you fool. We have someplace we need to be."

My father stood, a hearty laugh erupting from his very core. "My dear, you could not have accepted in a more appropriate fashion."

The moment was broken when they were snapped back to reality. Their first activity together as an engaged couple could turn out to be unpleasant. It would all depend upon how the Amos family reacted to the unplanned visit. He quickly got back into the buggy and continued their journey.

They arrived at the Amos farm, now a beautiful sight with a large house where the little shack had once stood, a manicured yard, fully mature tree groves bordering two sides of the property, a large barn, and fields of various crops beginning to sprout around it as far as the eye could see. He barely recognized the home he had grown up in. He was silent as they approached, though he could feel my mother's eyes on him. My father inhaled sharply, and then exhaled slowly, closing his eyes to steel himself for the events about to unfold. He pulled the buggy up to the hitching post near the barn and secured his team of horses before walking to my mother's side of the buggy and helping her out.

The house and large barn had been recently built. Cedric assumed that it must belong to his father. He wondered where the older of his brothers, who had taken over the farm, lived. He wondered where his other brother and his sister were now. In the distance, he saw the broad shoulders of his brother, Curtis, checking on the crops in the nearest field. He appeared much older than when they last met.

The tension in the air was electric. Both knew something monumental was about to happen regardless of the outcome of the visit. "Are you ready to meet the family, my love?" he asked. She nodded in response, though she looked unsure. The couple walked hand in hand towards the field. Curtis was bent over, inspecting a small corn plant, and failed to notice their approach. "Hello?" Cedric called.

Startled, Curtis stood and swung around. His look of surprise quickly turned to an angry scowl at seeing his visitors. "What are you doing here, and who is this with you?"

Cedric stood as still as a stone. "I came to introduce Father and the rest of you to my fiancée," Cedric stated calmly. His smile never faltered.

The angry look on Curtis' face changed to sheer rage. "Father? Have you been so busy with your own life that you have not heard? He passed away a month ago!"

My father gasped, "Father is gone?" he said in total disbelief.

"Yes!" roared Curtis. "He all but gave up after Mother passed away, and after you, his golden boy, could not be so much as bothered to come to her funeral! Let alone say nothing about our weddings or even show up around here once in a while!" The angry man stalked forward, closing the gap between them.

My father tried to speak but was quickly silenced by a large fist hitting the side of his face, knocking him to the ground. The door to the house burst open, and Francis, followed by his new bride, rushed out, prompted by the commotion. He stopped dead in his tracks, seeing my father lying on the ground. Rowena covered him with her own body, and Curtis stood over both of them, breathing heavily.

"Curtis? Is that... Cedric?" he asked, pushing his round glasses up his long, narrow nose. He moved his wife behind him as if to protect her with his lean body. "Who is that woman?"

Curtis was furious but had calmed enough to speak. "Yes, it is our *long-lost big brother*..." He drew out each word as he spoke, his words dripping with contempt. "He came to introduce *us* poor country folk and Pa to his fiancée."

"Pa?" He looked over at my father. "You didn't know?" Now Francis' face changed from calm to angry. Being more like my father, he did not yell. Instead, he just shook his head in disappointment. "You have not so much as visited since Mother passed. Now you want to come back here to show off your prize. You need to leave this property and never return." Though his voice was calm, his expression suggested that he could explode at any moment, like Curtis.

"Francis, Curtis..." my father started as he attempted to prop himself up in the grass.

"No, do not speak, just go," Francis stated.

"But I..." He started again, almost begging them to listen. As he did, Curtis raised a fist and advanced toward Cedric as if he was going to hit him again.

"Stop!" my mother screamed. "Cedric, get up! We are getting away from these madmen, brothers or not, now!" Her face was a mix of fear and fury. With that, she helped her fiancé to his feet, and they quickly advanced to the buggy, hand in hand.

My father held the side of his face where his brother had hit him. He was sure that he would have a sizable bruise the following day. My mother looked at him with concern. His only reply was a slight shake of his head, indicating that nothing needed to be said.

He unhitched his team of horses and drove his buggy away from his family home, sadness in his heart. The dust from the path that served as a driveway swirled around the occupants of the open buggy as they traveled away from the farm. He tried to pretend he was wiping dust from his eyes as he wiped away the tears. My mother turned her head, pretending not to notice as the thick silence seemed to engulf them. He never looked back. He stared straight ahead at the road home, unblinking, soundless, and seemingly lost in his thoughts.

After a while, she could no longer bear the silence, and the sadness which seemed to cover the buggy like a solid roof. She reached over and placed a gentle hand on my father's leg, causing him to jump a bit. He looked over at her briefly; eyes glazed, but still remained silent. He turned his attention back to the road without comment. She knew she had to break the silence. "Cedric, are you okay?"

Slowly, he looked her way again. "I cannot talk about this right now. Father is gone. My brothers hate me. I have no idea where my sister is. I have escaped from the farm, but at what cost?" He hung his head. She rubbed his leg but stopped herself before saying anything more, sensing it would only cause further issues.

The rest of the ride home was silent. The return to his home certainly had not gone as he had hoped it would, to say the least. There were no joyous embraces from his family. No welcome home. Not even congratulations on his engagement. Instead, he had been met by the reality that his father was gone. His siblings were married. Life had moved on without him. He came to the grim realization that he no longer had a family due to his own selfishness.

My father dropped my mother off that evening, sadness and regret continuing to engulf him. He knew they would eventually have to discuss what had happened, but tonight was not the time. The happiness they had felt from their engagement earlier in the evening was now a distant memory.

# Part 7: Fences to be Mended

Part 7: Fences to be Mended

Although the pain was still prominent, both physically and mentally, life needed to go on. My father opened the store the following day, and my mother came in to help as she did on any other day. Mother put on a brave face, acting as if the previous day had never happened. Although sadness hung in the air, she came into the store with a smile. "Hello, fiancé," she said as she kissed my father on the uninjured cheek. Father was relieved. She had not tried to talk about the previous day's event.

Her presence brightened his demeanor, and felt like a beam of sunshine breaking through the clouds of his sadness. "Good morning, my love," he said with a careful smile. The couple went about their day as usual. Beaming with joy, she proudly showed her new ring to each customer. My father tried to stay out of sight to avoid questions about his injury.

Everything was running smoothly until near the end of the day. The bell above the door rang one final time, and he turned to greet the customer with a smile.

There she was. His baby sister. No longer a baby, but all grown up. His smile turned to a look of surprise. She quickly closed the distance between them, raised her hand, and slapped him sharply across the face, hitting him directly across the same cheek their brother had bruised the previous day. My father gasped, grabbing his cheek.

My mother turned, hearing the impact. "Excuse me!" My mother exclaimed at the thin young woman standing before her fiancé. "Who are you, and why did you hit Cedric?"

Sissy stood, hands on hips, clearly frustrated and debating her next move. "I am his sister. You would be his fiancée, I presume?"

Startled, my mother stepped back and saw the family resemblance. Now, she also understood the reason for the slap. "Oh, my!" She exclaimed. She looked between the siblings.

My father looked ashamed. He pulled his hand away from his injured face and signaled to my mother that it was okay. "My Dear, would you mind giving us a few moments and locking the front door? Sissy and I are going to have a visit. It is close enough to closing time." He took a few steps towards the store office, hoping Mother would understand, and Sissy would follow. She nodded obediently, understanding that the two needed to clear the air.

My father escorted the angry Sissy to the office in the rear of the store and closed the door behind them. He sat down behind his desk carefully and motioned for Sissy to sit at the chair across from him. Instead, she paced side to side in the small office, seemingly too angry to sit, or speak. Finally, he spoke to her. "Sissy, I cannot possibly express how sorry I am." He hung his head as he finished the statement.

She stopped pacing, planting her hands firmly on the side of his desk. Her face was inches from his now. "You arrogant bastard!" Sissy seethed. "We all tried to tell you when Mother was getting ill. You ignored us. We saw you standing in the store as we passed during her funeral. You did not have enough respect for the woman who birthed and raised you to close the store and attend. Every time one of us needed supplies after that, you had someone else to wait on us. You were not there when your brothers got married. I got engaged to a wonderful man, and you have not even asked his name. You do not know where I live. Father has passed on. You will never know how proud he was of you and how your absence hurt him!" Sissy's cheeks became bright red as the tears streamed down her face. Her beautiful green eyes became bloodshot, and her long brown hair fell over her face.

He stood from his chair, and came around the desk, wrapping his arms around the small angry woman in a gentle embrace. She struggled momentarily against him, beating her fist against his chest, but then relented. He was also in tears. "Sissy, I'm *so* sorry. Words cannot express how incredibly sorry I am for all this. I wanted so badly to escape farm life and make a success of myself. All I ever wanted was to work in an actual business. I did not mean to hurt all of you. Can you *ever* forgive me?" The words tumbled out of his mouth so quickly that he was scarcely able to take a breath.

The two remained in their quiet embrace for quite some time, allowing the closeness of their bodies to mend what the years of separation had torn apart. Though the siblings knew things would never be the same, it was a start. When they finally stopped crying, the two looked at each other, observing the changes time had made on each of their faces. Gone was the youthful innocence that had once graced their faces. Now, in the place of the once smooth young skin, there were wrinkles. Had it really been that long?

Sissy's face became stoic as she spoke again. A bit of the tension from the previous conversation returned. "I can try to forgive you. I will not make any promises. As for our brothers, I am sure that will not happen. The first thing you need to do is to come with me to our parents' graves. You may not have been to their funerals, but you can at least have the respect to visit their graves. You need to ask for their forgiveness, regardless of whether they can answer. Pray that their spirits can hear you."

While drama unfolded only feet away, and curiosity tempted her, my mother had kept busy finishing up with closing the store. She had done her best not to eavesdrop, though when the yelling began; it was hard not to hear. She continued about her business respectfully, knowing how much of a milestone Aunt Sissy's visit was. When finished, she quietly exited the store, locking the door behind her. She rode home to her parents' farm, hoping that my father would be open to telling her what had happened later.

My father agreed that what he had been avoiding needed to be faced. He stopped to look around the store to ensure everything as it should be before they exited. He proudly noticed that everything was done as if he had closed it himself. His dear fiancée was a quick study and quite capable. She had left quietly, without disturbing him or his sister, earning his further respect. He made a mental note to compliment her regarding her competence.

The siblings walked silently and solemnly from the store to the cemetery at the far end of town. My father had not been there since his parents' death. Sissy led the way to the grave. The earth was still black and exposed, with only a few small blades of grass covering where Grandfather had been buried no more than a month ago. There was a wooden cross, a bit fancier than many of the others in the surrounding area, marking each parent's grave. They each bore the name of a parent, neatly carved, along with their dates of birth and death. An array of flowers was placed at their bases. It was clear that the graves were regularly visited and cared for.

He solemnly knelt in front of the graves. He silently vowed that a stone monument would be purchased from his own pocket. He had not been there for their funeral, but he was determined to do better for them in their afterlife. Tears silently flowed from his eyes. Sissy stood to his right, quietly watching the scene unfold. She observed his reaction and knew he was truly sorry for the last several years. Gently, she laid a hand on his shoulder, lending her support as he grieved.

"Mother, Father. I am so deeply sorry. I wanted so badly to be free of you. To be free of the farm. Now you are both gone," he sobbed.

Sissy silently squeezed his shoulder, closing her eyes and fighting back tears. From that moment on, the fences began to be mended between my father and Aunt Sissy. He raised his head and wiped his eyes. Sissy reached out a hand, helping him stand from the ground. He felt weak after releasing many years of pent-up emotion. The two once again embraced. At that moment, they both knew that despite all the hard feelings, there was a chance that they would once again have a relationship.

The two returned to the storefront, where they went their separate ways. My father did not go to my mother's home as he usually would. Instead he went directly home to process the day's events. That night, he sat alone at his table and stared at his sandwich. He had no appetite or desire to do anything other than go to sleep. Though he had done nothing physical, he was exhausted from the day's events. He lay down in bed, closed his eyes, and soon fell asleep.

"Cedric....Cedric......" The voice came. It was a familiar voice. His eyes were still closed. Where was it coming from?

He opened his eyes slowly and sat up in bed, looking around for the source of the voice. Nothing. He lay back down, thinking it must have just been the wind. Soon, the voice came again. This time, it was joined by another. "Wake up, my son!"

He sprang up in bed as if hit by a bolt of lightning. "Who is there?" He demanded, now wide awake.

Then he saw them. Two gray figures standing in the corner of his bedroom. He squinted his eyes as he reached for the small pistol he kept behind his pillow. Realization hit him. It was his father and mother. The difference was that they were not flesh and blood. They were...gray...solid, but gray... He gasped. "Who.... What...are you?" his voice quivered.

A voice came from the unmoving lips of the gray from of the man who appeared so similar to his father. "Be not afraid, my son," his father said. "We saw you visiting our graves today."

Cedric backpedaled as far as he could, hitting the wall in back of his bed with a thud. He pulled his blankets around him as tightly as he could. "I do not know who you are or why you are here. This must be a dream," he again stuttered, unable to believe his own eyes.

As if reading his mind, his mother began to speak. "You are not dreaming. We are here because we have been watching you," his mother replied, her gray face stern.

Fear, disbelief and sham overpowered him. "Have I really done anything so wrong? I made your farm successful and left to do what was best for me."

"That is only where the problem began," the gray man stated matter-of-factly. He pointed sharply at him. "You have forsaken your family and your roots. You were *never* present. Now, your siblings have moved on without you."

"I tried to go back..." his words trailed off. "I tried to apologize."

"It is too late. What you have done cannot be forgiven. For that, you and those who come after you are cursed..." His mother's voice seemed to fade. Then, before he could reason any further, they were gone.

He sat there on his bed, stunned. He had no idea what had just happened. Was it real, or was it somehow a very real dream? He shook his head, blinking rapidly and then climbed out of bed. The floor was cold on his bare feet. He knew that was real. He looked around the room. There was no one there. He walked to the window, and it was beginning to become light outside. He decided to try to forget about it, although a feeling of dread remained. He walked to his kitchen, and began to make himself a pot of coffee. He found himself continuously looking over his shoulder as he prepared for his day.

That day, my mother was already at the store waiting for him when he arrived. She did not speak, only smiled as he kissed her forehead. She knew him well enough to wait for him to be ready, and once he was, he would open up. Something felt off to her as they opened the store. She stole cautious glances at him as they worked, hoping he would not notice her concern. To their surprise, there were very few customers throughout the day, which allowed my father to explain the conversation he had with Aunt Sissy. He described in detail the visit to his parents' grave. Then, he reluctantly told her about his dream. My mother sat quietly and listened as he gave each detail. Now she knew what it was that had left him so upset.

He was visibly upset as he spoke. His voice shook. "It was just a dream, wasn't it?" he finally concluded.

She had an odd look on her face. She was unsure what to make of his story. Was it the stress? Had he actually experienced what he was describing? If he had, what did it mean? "Of course it was, dear. The dead cannot visit us once they are gone."

He wondered if she was holding something back, but did not comment. Several weeks went by before any of the Amos Family was seen again. This time, it was Uncle Curtis who made an appearance. He did not know what to expect as the large man entered the store. He watched silently as his brother stalked around the store, picking out needed supplies. No attempt was made to avoid the meeting. My father stood tall behind the counter of his store, my mother by his side. Everything appeared normal to anyone looking at the transaction from the outside, just a farmer visiting the local General Store for supplies. Only they knew how volatile the situation was.

Uncle Curtis laid the groceries down on the counter without a word. He rang up the purchase, and his only comment was the total cost. That was the end of their interaction.

As Uncle Curtis left the store, both my father and mother breathed a sigh of relief. No words had been spoken, yet a step in the right direction had been made. The siblings had been able to do business without any conflict. To him, it was a sign of hope.

Aunt Sissy became a regular fixture at the store. One day, she approached my father and asked if she could work part-time for him. He was a bit cautious; however, transferring more of the workload to employees would allow him and my mother more time together and more time to plan their wedding. Now, Sissy and my mother would have the chance to get to know each other and spend time together as their schedules allowed.

Sissy soon began working at the store, which also encouraged the uncles to come in more frequently. My father mainly began keeping tabs on the financials of all his stores rather than working in them. Aunt Sissy became the primary operator of the local store. My mother and father began traveling more, exploring new places for further growth.

My mother and Aunt Sissy discovered that they had many things in common as the two women became friends, so did my father and Aunt Sissy's fiancé, Gregory. Though bridges had not been completely mended, the brothers could again tolerate one another. There were tears of joy and laughter alike.

My parents wed, as did Aunt Sissy and Gregory, and for a time, life appeared happy. Yet somewhere in the back of his mind, the words I curse you and all those who come after you lingered, whispering to my father whenever he looked upon his bride, their fragile happiness, and the family he had begun to imagine.

# Part 8: Enter Cecil

Part 8: Enter Cecil

The rest of this story is my own. I hope that now that I have relayed my family's story, it may help you understand me a bit better.

My mother and father were happily married for just over a year. Business was booming at the store. He had begun speaking with his brothers and had gradually grown closer to Sissy. My mother and Sissy had also become best friends. Family dinners between the homes had become regular. It seemed that everything was aligning as it should. For the first time he could remember, Father was truly happy. He would not have changed anything in his life.

Almost exactly nine months after her wedding, Aunt Sissy had her first child. The little girl was the first child in the next generation of the Amos family. A little girl whom they named Violet. She was a beautiful bundle of joy; however, with her birth, Sissy needed to become a full-time mother. This left my father in a bit of a bind, for my mother was around five months pregnant with me. She had not been working in the store as much because the pregnancy had been difficult. She had been sick nearly every day and had been forced to spend a lot of time in bed as prescribed by the local physician. My father was forced to work long hours because he now had only one other reliable employee. The more difficult the pregnancy became, the larger the rift between them grew.

Most nights, my father woke up from dreams in a cold sweat. His lack of sleep further added to his exhaustion and frustration. Slowly, he was slipping back to the man he had been before she came into his life. He spent less and less time at home and more and more nights at the old apartment above his store. Alone, my mother could be heard weeping in her bed. This was not the life that he had promised her. Everything seemed to have changed.

Now, as Sissy was a new mother, my mother missed the companionship of her best friend. The wives of her two brothers-in-law visited occasionally to keep her company. She was able to be up for a short time but could not complete anything beyond the most minor tasks. The boredom was almost as unbearable as the pain of the pregnancy and the loneliness. Her main company was a shelf full of books that my father had collected. She allowed herself to escape to the different worlds the books drew her into. This eased the pain and boredom until the next time she was forced to move or to speak with someone.

My mother discovered what appeared to be a diary amongst the books on the shelf. The handwriting was familiar, and she recognized it as my father's. She knew she should not have read it, but she longed for him and felt it a way to be close to him. In the diary, she discovered the stories of his early years. How much he had hated growing up on the farm. He also went into detail about his growing resentment for my grandfather. She had heard him tell these stories before, but had never known the extent of them. She was beginning to understand what had happened between my father and his family. She feared she had been selfish. She began to feel sorry for him and softened to the current situation.

Then, one day, she stumbled across something she had never heard before: my grandmother's lineage. My father had gone into detail about each of his parents, telling their story. He had written extensively about his mother, telling him stories about where she came from and her customs. Even some of the magic she claimed to possess. He wrote that she would say each meal she made had a bit of magic. She told him as a young child that if he were not good, she would curse him and turn him into one of the farm animals he hated. That would teach him to treat them with respect. He also wrote about the happy memories of her singing in her foreign tongue as she worked. All these were things she had never known before.

As she read, she heard the door open. She quickly hid the diary beneath her pillow and awaited my father's entry. Disappointment flooded over her weary mind and body. As he neared, she could smell the alcohol. He had been drinking heavily. His words were slurred as he spoke to her. "Hello, darlink." My mother reacted quickly and rolled as far to the side as she could, protecting her very pregnant stomach with both hands. He fell onto their bed, narrowly avoiding landing atop her, and immediately passed out. Disappointment turned to hurt as she realized that mixed with the smell of stale alcohol was the smell of another woman's perfume. She began to silently weep. What had their lives together become? Was he truly that miserable that he had turned to the company of another woman while she was pregnant? This pregnancy was supposed to be a thing of joy. A hope for the future. Not something that made her miserable, and drove her beloved away.

That night, my father slept soundly, but my mother was the one who awoke to a woman she did not recognize standing at the foot of her bed. The woman was not fully solid but resembled the coloration of a stone statue. My mother was startled and attempted to shake my father awake, but received only a deep snore in response. The 'stone woman' smiled gently. "Do not worry, my child. I will not harm you. I am here only to warn you. You have been reading about me."

Instantaneously, she realized that this was her long-dead mother-in-law. How could it be? The woman appeared to flicker a bit.

"I come bearing a warning. Your husband is not the man I had hoped he would become. I raised him to love his family and wife. Instead, he continues to fall back on his old ways of pursuing money. Since money is all that matters to him, I have cursed him and any of his line to a life with no happiness aside from what money can bring." Then she was gone.

My mother fell back against her pillow, fainting from the shock of what she had just experienced. When she awoke the following day, my father was already gone. Odds were that he would not believe her story anyway. She briefly recalled a story he had told her long ago, about a similar experience he had. If she mentioned it, would he remember, and believe her, or would it just anger him? She had no one to talk to about her experience, so she kept it to herself.

As ill as she was, she had time, and writing would become her way of passing the long, dull days. My mother began keeping her own journal. Should something ever happen to her, there would be records. She found an empty pad of paper and started writing her story. She spent hours writing down memories from as far back as she could remember. Finally, she detailed the recent dream while it was still clear in her memory.

Self-preservation, and love for her unborn child took over. She had other things to worry about. She knew she had to keep herself healthy for the next few months. She had no idea if her marriage would ever be the same, and now she suspected that my father had returned to his previous drunken womanizing ways.

The rest of the pregnancy passed in a very similar fashion. Doctors' visits became daily, and my mother became entirely bedridden, with a nurse staying in the house now instead of my father. Then the day came. It was the day of a solar eclipse. My mother had labored throughout the night. My father eventually grew tired of his wife's pained howling and left to go to the store. I was born after an unusually long and complicated labor at the moment when the sky was darkest.

From the moment I was born, it was clear that I was a handsome boy. I looked much like my father, with a full head of dark hair, apparent high cheekbones, and fair skin. My mother, though in a horrendous amount of pain, held me briefly with a proud smile, and then she blacked out. The attention was taken away from me, as I was healthy and crying. I was hastily cleaned up, and then placed in a bassinet. Attention was returned to my mother, who appeared to be quickly fading away.

My father was retrieved from his store despite his protest. The doctor insisted he come home as his wife's life was hanging in the balance, and he needed to be there should she pass away. At that, his demeanor changed, and he hurried to their shared home. My mother survived after a long evening of medical care from the doctor. It was discovered after she awoke that the birth had taken its toll. She could not feel her legs. She had been rendered paralyzed and barren after my birth. The brief happiness surrounding my birth was shattered at the discovery. Questions plagued both of their minds. Mother was exhausted after the physical struggle of giving birth. Now there was an additional complication. Even with a wheelchair, would she be able to take care of her newborn son or complete even the most basic tasks around the home? Father sobered quickly, realizing their plight. He paced the room, hands crossed behind his back, brooding. Mother called out to him, but he refused to reply. He was lost in his own world. Their already strained marriage now seemed doomed.

Father was thrilled to have an heir. However, he had no idea how he was going to handle a disabled wife, a new baby, and a business. He stopped pacing briefly, staring at his wife holding their new baby. Suddenly, he remembered the 'dream' where his mother had appeared to him and the curse she had placed on him. The words: "If money is all that matters to you, I curse you, and any of your line which may come after you to a life with no happiness aside from what money can bring!" Could this be a result? He shook his head trying to clear the thought.

Mother paid him no attention. She was overjoyed at my birth. She quickly healed and adapted to her new life as a disabled mother. Ever the positive type, she refused to let her new disability dampen her joy. She ignored her own pain, and made every effort to recover as much of her independence as she could. She learned to use her wheel chair, and worked at strengthening her arms so that she did not have to ask for help any more often than absolutely necessary. She could see Father spiraling further, yet she held out hope that she could somehow salvage what was left of what they had once had. I became the bright spot in the darkness of her days. It seemed that I was giving her the will to keep going on although world seemed to have crumbled around her.

Despite her best efforts, everything she could do was not enough. She still required assistance. My mother's needs became too much for my father. He hired a woman to help around the house and with a newborn me. My father's absence became more prominent. He could not handle the stress, the pain, and the depression that sprang from it. The demons of his past, which had begun to rear their ugly heads during the past nine months, now overtook him. Alcoholism had only been temporarily concealed during the brief bliss of the new relationship. He had now fully withdrawn from his wife and me. He was constantly on the move and cared about nothing but his empire.

He hired someone full-time to run the local store. He could not face what had happened to his beautiful wife and what had become of their happiness. To him, everything else seemed beyond his control. He blamed himself for wanting an heir. Had Rowena never met him, she might have had a full, happy life. Guilt overwhelmed him more with each day.

It felt as though the order of his world was unraveling. To save his reputation, he tried to hide what was happening from the rest of the world. After all, with him traveling, who would ever know if he drank too much and warmed his bed with whatever attractive woman would have him? When he did come home, he did his best to appear the husband he had once been. Soon, my father and mother were married only by name and reputation. They slept in separate rooms and barely spoke. To the public, the marriage still appeared happy. In the secrecy of our home, he became more and more angry and abusive.

My mother made things work with the help of our hired staff. I grew quickly. I was healthy and strong. I was much like my father in that I was very smart. From an early age, I knew he resented me for what had happened to my mother. I had rendered his beautiful Rowena unable to bear more children or able to walk again. He did not look at me with adoration as my mother did. He never held me or played with me. He spoke to me in only cold, stern tones. I knew something was different between him and me. It made me question whether this was how all fathers were with their children. Was it common for them to be absent most of the time? As my mother was wheelchair-bound, we rarely left home, so as a young child, I did not have any friends, thus no other families to compare my own to.

My father knew I was the only heir and the only hope for the Amos Empire to continue. This triggered a mix of emotions within him. As I grew up, this was made very clear to me. At school age, I began to understand. We were different from other families.

There were things that were expected of me as the heir. I was to be responsible. I was not to do anything other than go to school and learn the family business. I was never to speak of what went on under our roof's privacy. I was always to be respectful to my father when he was present and never to question him.

# Part 9: Cecil Begins to Mature

My mother was kind despite her situation. She loved me with all her heart and was never cruel to me. In my eyes, she was an angel. I had no idea how she was able to cope with the hand life had dealt her and love the person who was, in large part, responsible.

Because of my father's controlling nature, I only glimpsed her true personality as I grew up. More often, I saw the woman who had been terrified into submission by someone she had once trusted. When he was present, he was a tyrant. His rules were always to be followed. She felt trapped and did her best to maintain the appearance of a perfect wife in public. I felt confused. As I grew up, I could see how miserable she was.

She was still beautiful even after birthing me and losing mobility in her legs, though she always appeared to be tired and sickly. She spent the majority of her time cooking and cleaning as best she could, when she was not tending to me. She never spoke ill of him when we were in public—only bragged about his successes. She never complained about her position in life. She always took great care of me and taught me to read before I went to school. While I worked hard to learn, I observed that my mother enjoyed reading and was often found writing in a notebook. I was not allowed to read what she had written and was told that it was her journal and was never to be read by anyone. I soon realized that writing was her escape. It was what was keeping her sane. When she wrote, I often observed that her gaze appeared far away and dreamy. I wondered what she was dreaming of and where she tried to escape.

I had inherited intelligence from both my mother and father and enjoyed learning. No physical work or chores of any kind were expected of me. I knew I would someday be expected to be in the same business as my father. This made my world predictable, yet I dreamt of what else may be out there besides what he had planned for me. When he was home, he talked to me about the family business as if I were already an adult. I dared not pay him anything less than full attention as he spoke. The sad realization came to me that I had no reason to allow my mind to dream or wander. I would be what he intended, whether I wanted to or not.

I noticed that my parents were very different from the other children's parents. When I was a young child, in public, I was forced to hold my father's hand as my mother rolled along beside me on the opposite side in her wheelchair. To the outside world, we would have appeared to be a happy family, aside from my mother's disability.

At home, the differences were prominent. The feeling was never that of a happy home. It was a continually tense environment. I never knew when to expect an argument or just tense silence. My parents rarely spoke or touched. My mother explained to me, when I was old enough to realize, that my father traveled a lot for work, so he was rarely home. When she did speak, he quickly interrupted her, shutting down anything she had to say and making sure to keep her in what he felt was her proper place. She would lower her head and immediately stop speaking.

I would often hear them arguing while I pretended to be asleep in bed. The next day, she would do her best to hide some sort of bruise. The bruises were always on a limb, never on her face. This ensured that the injuries were easily hidden from anyone who might cause the prominent family trouble over such matters. After all, they could not afford a scandal tarnishing *his* reputation.

As I grew into a teenager, I was well aware of what was happening within our home. My father was not just away on business; he was with other women. My mother was left alone to raise their only child and fend for herself. I began to quietly resent him for hurting the sweet woman who was my mother. I loved her deeply and would have done anything to protect her. I admired her courage and her commitment to the family's reputation. I respected her but did not understand why she tolerated his poor treatment.

I studied hard and was the brightest student in school. Unlike my father before me, I was encouraged to stay in school, which thrilled me as I enjoyed absorbing knowledge. I hoped my parents would allow me to continue in college before officially forcing me to join the family business. I began to dream of a world outside of the family business once again.

The girls my age in my small school all knew of the wealth my family had amassed. Between wealth, my handsome appearance, and my intelligence, they all seemed to pine for me. I had no interest in courting any of the young available women. I did not want to take the risk of anything keeping me stuck here. I had begun to hate my home environment. I hated what I was seeing. I hated how my mother simply accepted her circumstances and quit dreaming as things had worsened in her life. I hated what I was expected to become. I knew for certain that I did not want my own life to turn out like either of my parents' lives. For now, I would follow what was expected to appease my father.

The seed of an escape dream had begun to sprout in my head. The only detour I faced with the sprouting dream was my fear of leaving my mother. My mother and learning were the driving forces in my life. The things that kept me of sound mind. I felt I needed to protect her from my father as long as I could. I did not know what would happen to her once I left.

One fateful night, my worst nightmare came true. When he was home, the fighting was loud enough to wake me. I realized that it was a loud crash that had awoken me. I heard them yelling. My mother screamed. I sat up in my bed, startled. I slid my legs over the side of my bed, tiptoed to the door, and opened it slowly, ensuring it did not make a sound. I opened it just enough to slip out. I moved slowly and silently to the opposite side of the house, to my mother's bedroom. The door was cracked slightly. I silently peeked through. The site that met my eyes was nothing less than terrifying.

My Father stood over her, breathing heavily, fists clenched tightly. She lay crumpled in the corner, quietly sobbing, wheelchair tipped beside her, one wheel still slowly rotating.

Suddenly, I was overcome by anger. I burst through the door and surged towards my father. Before he could react, I grabbed his arm, struggling to push the much larger man away from my beloved mother. In that moment, our eyes met. His cold blue eyes now appeared to be a shade of dark gray. They were filled with surprise and anger. I had managed to push him back slightly.

It was as if I were seeing my actions through someone else's eyes. My movements came without thought, only instinct. My hands were locked firmly on his forearms as we wrestled violently for control. I could not focus on both him and my mother at the same time. I managed to crane my head her way for a moment. Tears streamed down her face. I could hear her begging my father not to hurt me. I saw her struggle to sit up out of the corner of my eye. Her pain was apparent. I felt torn, wanting to help her from the ground, yet prevailed. I wanted nothing worse at that moment than to hurt that man as badly as he had hurt my mother. All of the years as a helpless bystander seemed to be compounded into this very moment. Hadn't this man done enough to hurt her already?

In that brief moment, I became distracted, and it was too late. He took advantage of his larger size, pulled his arm loose from my grasp, and shoved me. I hit the wall with a thud, and the world went black.

I had no idea how much time had elapsed when I awoke on the floor. My mother, now back in her wheelchair, sat by my side. The housemaid was dabbing at my forehead with a cold cloth. I opened my eyes slowly. My head throbbed. I raised my hand, gingerly touching the back of my head. I pulled my hand away, alarmed by the warm, sticky feeling. I realized that the back of my head was bleeding and remembered what had happened.

My father stood on the other side of the room, quietly staring out the window with his hands folded behind his back. The wave of anger came back. I tried to stand, but she raised her hands, signaling me to stop and shaking her head no. The pain in her eyes said what she could not voice. I felt myself calm marginally. As she watched my eyes calm, she did not object as I eased myself into an upright position. I allowed her to guide me slowly back to my room. She bandaged my bleeding head and then pulled the covers up over my shoulders as I tried to get comfortable. Considering my age, I felt a bit silly at the treatment; however, I allowed it due to the night's events. Perhaps helping me would, in some way, help her as well.

The next day, for the first time I could recall, I did not attend school. My injury served as my father's justification for keeping me home; he feared questions, feared the conclusions drawn from what could be seen. But the town required no evidence. Rumors had already taken root. They spoke openly of Cedric Amos's wealth and his ceaseless travels, as though absence itself were an admission of guilt. They speculated about his sickly wife, about which of her needs might be met beyond the walls of our home. They cast knowing glances at my mother's long sleeves and modest dress, measuring what they imagined she concealed. And then there were the questions about me—why I was so silent, why I showed no interest in young ladies, why I seemed so unlike other boys. In their eyes, our household was not merely peculiar, but suspect. The weight of their suspicions churned in my stomach, leaving me ill with the certainty that we were already judged.

My resentment for my father grew with each passing moment. I loathed him. I wanted out. I knew I had no choice but to stay as long as possible, if nothing else, for my mother's sake.

I knew I was expected to take over the business. I also knew the business had many locations, and my father continually sought to expand his empire. The dream of moving on had not dimmed for me. With recent events, it had grown stronger, if nothing else. My hope was that my father requiring me to travel for business, would eventually allow me an out.

My uncles and my aunt had once again almost wholly stopped communicating with my father due to his behavior. They knew what was going on, and even Aunt Sissy, my mother's best friend, was unable to get her to admit she was being abused. I was the only person who had witnessed it and held the burden of proof. I, however, had a secret of my own.

I had been visiting the Amos Family farm whenever I could and learning as much as I could from my uncles about the farm business. Although I loved business and enjoyed my schoolwork, I discovered that I also enjoyed working with my hands. Plus, I knew my father would hate the thought of me doing something he despised so much.

I became further intrigued as I learned how much accounting went into keeping a farm profitable. A farmer had to know how to live off the money made once or twice a year for the rest of the year. They needed to know which crops grew best on their land, which crops sold best, and when to sell them. They also needed to understand which animals sold well and at what weight. All those factors need to be balanced with the need to keep enough supplies on hand to care for one's family. Then there were the expenses associated with the everyday running of a farm. If I were to take farming as a trade, I could have the best of both worlds: business and being in the great outdoors. Plus, I would be hurting my father in the worst way possible.

I was exhausted, but wholly satisfied as I came home late and dirty from working on the farm. I knew my father was not to be home. I had been guarding my secret carefully. It had become increasingly harder with the close relationship my mother and I had always shared. I had thought it through. This would be the night I would share my plan with her. Mother sat at the kitchen table writing in her journal. She looked at me with curiosity as I entered our home. I smiled, and engulfed her in my sweaty embrace. She giggled at me, asking what I had gotten myself into. I disclosed my newfound love to my mother that evening. To my surprise, she did not object. She was happy for me, although weariness showed through her smile. She wanted to ensure that I experienced all the things in life that I wanted to, rather than just committing to taking over the family business. We agreed to keep the secret from my father so that I could continue visiting my relatives. I would only do so when we could confirm that he was out of town. The secret further deepened my bond with my mother as it was something that only we shared.

Being around my family improved my disposition. I loved my aunt and uncles. I really loved playing with Uncle Curtis's first child, a new baby boy. I was becoming less withdrawn. I smiled and spoke with the people I met at our store in town, especially the farmers, instead of merely tolerating their presence. I visited with them and learned. I let them know how much I admired and respected what they did. Without so many words, I made it very clear that I was not my father, only his son. My schedule was very full. I enjoyed working in the store and in school. I enjoyed my time on the Amos farm the most. However, the physical work tanned my skin, toughened my hands, and built muscle in my lean body. When I had the opportunity to look at myself in the mirror one afternoon, I barely recognized myself. I loved the effects. I began to look more like my father's brothers than I did him. Unfortunately, the bone structure in my face, jet-black hair, and blue eyes were still identical to my father's. I cut my hair shorter to avoid wearing it the way my father did, and I often hid it beneath a hat.

What the family did not know was that the experience on the farm was leading to my next chapter in life.

# Part 10: The Business Trip

Part 10: The Business Trip

As I matured and my father aged, he began to slow down. He traveled less but still did not spend much time at home. He stayed in the area and began sending me on longer business trips after I graduated high school. These trips were needed to keep up with the business's expansion and ensure the existing stores ran smoothly. He also expected that I would visit the colleges in the area where I was sent to consider where I wanted to continue my education before fully taking over Amos Enterprises. I dutifully followed these requirements, all the while keeping my dream in mind. I reviewed each location as a potential escape route.

I continued to visit the farm when possible. I knew I needed to be very cautious in doing so. My mother became increasingly frail, but I knew she was in good hands with the nurse who now lived in a small cottage near our house and the wonderful housekeeper. When my father stayed at home, I made sure that I was there as much as possible so that he could not harm her without my knowing. I was larger than him now and much younger. As long as I was at home, I could make sure he did not touch her.

I kept my communication with my father to a minimum. At the supper table on a warm summer evening in June, he announced that he had a job for me to do.

He sat his fork down on his plate with a clang, and cleared his throat as if to ensure my mother and I were paying attention. "Son, the time has come for you to take a bigger role in this business. There is much potential for growth in the Midwest. Things are beginning to settle down and become a bit safer there now. I want to expand Amos Enterprises into a location, or possibly multiple locations, in that area. I am too old to travel that far now. You must travel there instead and decide if expansion could be profitable."

This was an unexpected turn of events. I was caught off guard, and unsure how to feel about being forced to travel so far. I opened my mouth to protest.

He slammed his fist on the wooden table, seeing that I was about to object. "Silence! The decision has been made! The tickets have already been purchased!

You will leave next week. That will give me time to hire someone to care for the store in your absence." My father smiled wickedly, his cold blue eyes gleaming.

I seethed, trying to think of something to come back with, but for the moment, I was stumped for a response. I stared at the old man, mulling over the situation. I considered attending a business school, but the Midwest had never crossed my mind. My home was on the East Coast, and there were many good colleges. My escape plan had encompassed moving, but never that far. This trip would delay my plans. It was as if my father was well aware, though neither my mother nor I had disclosed anything to him. Had he somehow found out?

His resentment for me showed clearly as he glared in my direction. At that moment, looking into those wicked eyes, a thought formed. As far as I was aware, he knew nothing of my interest in farming. Therefore, he had not considered that the Midwest was a rich farming center. This may be the perfect opportunity for me. He was giving me the perfect opening without even knowing. I did not comment. I just sneered back at him, my contempt matching his own. My mother looked between us, sensing the tension, then broke the silence.

"Cecil. Just think. This will allow you to see the country. Maybe you can visit some business schools as you travel," her voice was weak.

I turned to her, my face softening. I reached across the table and brushed her gaunt face lightly with the back of my hand. I knew that she was aware of where my thoughts were wandering. "Yes, Mother. You are correct. It will be a great learning experience, as well as an adventure."

I packed during the following week. By the time I was through, most of my belongings were in one large cedar chest. The necessities were in a satchel, always to be by my side. My father gave me directions on where to get on the train and how many stops it would take to reach my destination. He provided me with cash and a checkbook bearing the name Amos Enterprises. Lastly, he handed me a small revolver, which he had always kept with him, advising me to keep it hidden unless I intended to use it.

I checked with the husband of my mother's nurse to ensure that he kept a close watch on her when my father was home and instructed him not to hesitate to get the Sheriff should he so much as touch her. I also spoke to my uncles and ensured that they checked in on them frequently, regardless of how my father felt. I was prepared and ready for the adventure to begin.

It was time for me to leave. I stood in the doorway of the only home I had ever known and took a look around, memories of the good and bad moments of my life flashing through my memory. I kissed my mother gently and held her hand for a long time, not knowing when I would see her again. Seeing the emotional display, my father quickly intervened, rushing me out the door and into the waiting vehicle. He drove us to our destination, looking dapper in his best suit. The impression left on the public who watched curiously was that the next generation of the Amos family was taking the reins of the business. I respectfully bowed to him, never touching or exchanging words, but ensuring that the public appearance was kept. At that, I boarded the train with my satchel over my shoulder. My trunk had been loaded in a different car with the rest of the luggage. None of the emotion I had felt at leaving my mother present as I looked at him through the window of the train. I smiled feeling the slightest bit of relief, and hope that this trip would be the beginning of my freedom.

The large black train lurched forward, with smoke billowing out of the stack near the front of the engine. Chug – chug – chug – chug – whoooo-whoooooo... I was pitched forward in my seat as the engine came to life, slowly moving the cars toward their destination. I took one last look at him standing there, and then turned and faced the seat in front of me. I closed my eyes, inhaling deeply. I was hopeful that I could find a purpose out in the Midwest. Maybe stake a claim of my own instead of just being Cecil Amos, son of Cedric Amos. I allowed myself to relax in my seat as a slight feeling of relief washed over me.

The journey between the East Coast and the Midwest took 4 days. Though the country was still wild, the railroad had an effect. My only thoughts of home were thoughts of my family. I found myself excited, rather than home sick although I did miss Mother and my aunt and uncles. There were many train stations along the way. I took the opportunity to curiously explore each town at each stop. I also purchased some small tokens from each stop where a store sold anything other than essential goods. I collected barrettes for my mother and fine combs. I managed to find some perfume for my aunts, a doll for Violette, and toys for the baby. For my uncles, I bought each a pocketknife with fine bone handles. Each item was added carefully to my travel trunk for its future owner.

Because of my social standing, I was able to keep a window seat whenever the train stopped at a new station. The journey seemed long and tedious.

Thankfully, the company changed multiple times throughout the journey, and there were no robberies. The ocean from the East Coast was replaced by forests, streams, and lakes. The closer I got to my destination, the flatter the landscape was. The grass itself sometimes resembled a flowing sea of green. In fact, the last leg of the journey was relatively uneventful. There was the occasional hill, but no more mountains.

I became nervous and excited as I neared my final destination. I changed from my business clothes to plain slacks and a shirt. Now, I looked like any other common person getting to their destination. I patted the satchel, ensuring my pistol was still there. I made sure to hide the money and the checks in the hidden compartment my mother had sewn into the satchel for me before my departure. I hoped I would not need to use the revolver. The Midwest had tamed some during the early part of the twentieth century; however, it was still a much more dangerous place than my home. Aside from a short nap, I was unable to sleep during the last leg of my journey.

I peered out the window as the town came into view. I waited patiently for the train to come to a stop. I was anxious to begin my new adventure. The destination, a small town called Pheasant's Crossing, was finally reached. It was much smaller than the town I had come from, but by all appearances, it was clean and well-kept. I was deposited at the train station on Main Street, and my trunk was unloaded. I was near the local hotel, which I was grateful for. I grunted as I picked up the large trunk, my biceps and chest straining. I lugged it into the lodgings and set it down with a thud. I took a look around the meager motel, observing the unpainted walls, small wooden desk, and plain wooden plank floor. It was clean, but much less grand than what I was used to.

As I approached, I was greeted by a kind-looking woman at the front desk. "Hello, how may I help you, sir?" she asked with a courteous smile.

I flashed my most charming smile, determined to make a good first impression on the first person I interacted with in my new home town. "Good evening, Ma'am. My name is Cecil Amos. I am in need of lodging for an extended stay. Do you happen to have a room available?"

"Pleasure to meet you, Mr. Amos. We do have a room available. How long do you intend to stay with us?"

I thought for a moment, unsure how to respond. A time frame had not been set for this trip. "At this time, I am unsure. I am here on business. May I start with renting your fine accommodations for a week?"

"Certainly, sir."

With that, I was directed to a room on the second floor, and a key was handed to me. The woman at the front desk smiled as I flipped my satchel towards my back and once again hefted the large chest. Though she was much older, she could not seem to take her eyes off me as I made my way to my room. Once in my room, after placing my trunk full of belongings in a corner, I collapsed onto the bed and was almost immediately asleep.

For the first time since the beginning of my trip, I slept soundly through the night. I was comfortable, safe, and ready to meet my father's potential new business partner tomorrow.

I awoke, refreshed. To my surprise, the hotel had a basin of fresh water for me to groom myself. I gladly dipped the provided cloth into the basin and cleaned all the dirt from my skin. I then shaved the days-old stubble from my face. When I finished, I went to the window and looked out. There did not appear to be anyone beneath my room, so I opened the window, leaned my head out, and dumped the remaining water over my head, vigorously rubbing my thick, dark hair. I shook the remaining water from my hair and pulled my head back into the room. I stretched my arms above my head, yawning. I smiled at the fresh scent of the air. It's much different than the air back home.

I dressed in the best suit I had in preparation to find Mr. Frederick Stingle. I checked my appearance in the mirror, realizing I looked like a different man than the one who had entered the hotel the previous day. My dark hair was clean and slicked back; I was freshly shaved and wore a suit rather than plain slacks and a shirt. I squared my shoulders and stepped confidently out of my door. The woman who had checked me in the previous evening was again at the front desk.

"Excuse me, Ma'am."

The older lady flushed as she looked up and saw my smiling face.

"Yes..., How may I help you..., Mr. Amos?"

"Why, you remember my name. I am honored," my smile grew.

"Yes, Sir. I make it a practice to know all my patrons."

"Do you happen to know where I can find a Mr. Fredrick Stingle?"

"Why, yes. Mr. Stingle owns the General store. He should be there now. It is just down the street to the right from here."

Armed with the information I needed, I thanked the friendly lady and went to find him. I whistled my favorite tune as I walked down the road toward the store. To my surprise, its appearance was very similar to the one back home, except it was smaller and looked slightly in disrepair. The front bore the same plate-glass windows as our store, one of which had a large spiderweb-like crack running across it. It had a wooden overhang and sidewalk. The storefront was faded, as was the painted sign bearing its owner's name. The faded red paint now appeared closer to pink. The door itself seemed to be barely clinging to its hinges.

I cautiously grabbed the rusty door handle and pulled the rickety door open. It squeaked in protest. I paused for a moment, looking around at my new surroundings. Despite the building's slightly run-down exterior, the interior was tidy. The shelves were full and well-organized. I was pleased with what I saw.

Behind the front counter stood a balding middle-aged man. He looked up from his paper and greeted me warmly. "Good morning. How can I help you today, young fella?" He was short and somewhat pudgy.

I cleared my thro tans spoke clearly and confidently. "Good morning, Sir. I am Cecil Amos, the son of Cedric Amos. May I presume that you are Mr. Stingle?"

The older man chuckled. "No need to be so formal, son. Yes. I'm Fred. Nice to meet you."

We continued to visit for a while. I truly liked the older man. We looked over the store's books, and to my surprise, it was making money. I could see no reason not to tell my father to expand to this location. The next day, I was allowed to observe the store from the office so I could meet some locals and see what the community was like.

I enjoyed watching the customers come and go. The customers here were mostly farmers. There were no businessmen or fancy suits, as was common at home. I felt like I had found somewhere I could walk away from the life I had at home and strike out on my own. I found myself falling in love with the fresh, dusty air. I liked everyone I met. No one treated me as if I were being judged.

They all just greeted me, and I visited with each of them. They treated me as if I were welcome.

# Part 11: FATE

Part 11: FATE

On what was to be the last day of my visit, one of the farmers asked me to join him and his family for an evening meal. I found the idea of a home-cooked meal very appealing after eating at the local restaurant during my entire visit. Little did I know that a simple meal would point me in the direction of the future that I had been looking for. I rode out to the farm alongside the friendly farmer in the noisy Ford and upon arriving, was pleased to see a small white house that looked very welcoming.

As we walked into the house, I stopped, closed my eyes, and inhaled deeply. The scent of freshly baked bread mixed with meat and vegetables left my mouth watering. "Indeed, this is wonderful! Thank you so much for the invitation," I warmly told my host.

He slapped me on the back and smiled, thrilled that I was pleased with his humble home. "Well, come on in and have a seat until supper's ready." He led me to the sitting area, where I took a seat. He went to the kitchen, and I could hear a muffled conversation between my new friend and an unknown female, who I assumed was his wife. He returned, and we had a short discussion.

As I turned my head, I found myself frozen. I saw the most beautiful creature I had ever imagined. She carried a platter of meat surrounded by potatoes and carrots. She reminded me very much of a younger version of my beloved mother. Her hair was long, blonde, and wavy. She was taller than most women, with broad shoulders, long, well-toned legs, and womanly curves in all the right places. I was speechless, stunned by her beauty.

"Cecil, this is my daughter, Matilda," my host proudly stated. She was followed by the older, almost identical version of herself. "This is my wife, Mildred."

I turned back to my friend with a mischievous grin. "You are a lucky man, John."

Matilda and Mildred blushed and giggled a bit.

John sat at one end of the table, and myself on the other, the women on either side. Conversation flowed freely throughout dinner. I could not keep my eyes off Matilda; the feeling seemed mutual. Every time I looked up from my plate, our eyes met. It was at that precise moment that I knew I was going to ask this beautiful girl for a date. My decision to tell my father to buy the store was now clearer than ever. It was the most pleasant evening I had experienced since my arrival. I did not want the evening to end. Alas, I knew it had to. As the meal concluded, the women cleared the table, and the men sat near the fireplace visiting about nothing in particular. On the ride home, I gathered all of my bravery, and nervously asked John if I may take his daughter out on an evening in the near future. To my delight he smiled at me, and stated. "I was hoping you would ask."

I could barely sleep due to excitement that night. Immediately upon waking, I dressed as quickly as I could and headed to the telegram office. I knew I needed to buy myself some further time with Matilda. I thought weighed my options carefully. I had been sent here to make a determination on if a location here would be profitable or not. I determined my best option would be to tell a white lie. I sent my father a telegram advising him that I needed more time to research the store and its location before making a decision. I extended my stay using funds from the account sent to me. After I completed that task, I needed to talk to Mr. Stingle. He needed to know that I was not reneging on the deal, only extending my stay a bit longer before closing on it. With a spring in my step I walked from the telegram office to the store, whistling. Upon arrival, I explained to the friendly shop keeper that I now had further reason to establish roots in Pheasant's Crossing.

To the surprise of John, Mildred and Matilda, my next stop was their home. , I showed up in plain clothes instead of my business suit and pitched in with the farm work. They were glad for the help, and impressed that I was not afraid to get dirty. Not only that, but I had knowledge of what needed to be done, and required little instruction. From that day forward, instead of spending time at the store, I spent my time at the farm of the beautiful Matilda and her family. After each workday, Matilda and I were allowed to do as we pleased.

We spent the next week finding quiet places to spend time alone on the farm. We enjoyed getting to know each other. We seemed to have a lot in common. She was brilliant, loved to read, and enjoyed school. She was also an only child, and her mother was also unable to have more children for reasons unknown. Unlike me, her upbringing had been pleasant and happy.

My newfound farmer friend was a doting father; his beautiful daughter was his pride and joy. Her parents had spoiled her however they could, despite not having much money.

Matilda was as sweet as honey and as innocent as a lamb. She dreamt of becoming a farm wife, settling down, and having a family with a man she loved. Little did she know our dreams aligned! I had never thought much about a wife, much less children. This beautiful young woman changed all that. I wanted to give her the life she desired. I pictured finding a piece of land, building a house and a barn, buying animals, and breaking ground for the farmland. I pictured working hard during the day to coax a bountiful harvest from the land and carefully tending the animals. I pictured a wedding in the loft of the barn we would build with my family, her family, and all our friends. I dreamt of a white house with a little picket fence around the front, a large kitchen, and plenty of room for a growing family. I dreamt of leaving the life of a businessman and blazing my own trail in the Midwest, leaving behind the violent home life and returning to my roots. I wanted to be like my uncles and my grandparents before them. To have a loving family of my own. Nothing like my father.

My mother, who had been such a shining example of a loyal wife and an outstanding mother, had given me an idea of what I wanted my future to look like without my knowing it. I had spent hours dreaming about what she would have been like had she not become paralyzed during my birth. I could not give her back her life, but I could give my wife the life that she desired. That was within my power. I had made up my mind what I wanted. I just hoped that Matilda would want it, too.

The time had come for me to return home. I could no longer continue the ruse with my father. He had begun to ask questions, and I had finally had to give him the news that I had deemed the store worthy to purchase, and set a return date. On the last evening of my visit, Matilda and I lay in an alfalfa field surrounded by the sweet smell of its flowers. The mood was somber as we lay side by side, hand in hand, looking up at the stars and breathing in the cool evening air.

"I do not want you to go," she spoke softly.

"I must," I sighed and looked away.

I knew we had only been seeing each other for a short time, but I felt the time was right. I somehow knew what the answer to my next question would be before I asked. I propped myself on one elbow and smiled at the young woman I had fallen in love with. I reached my free hand up and caressed her face. "What if I had a plan?" I asked with a glint in my eye.

"A plan for what, Cecil?" she asked, her confusion evident.

"A plan for me to return and make you my wife." The confidence she would say yes was apparent in my tone.

She sprang up quickly. "Are you asking me what I think you are?" Her eyes welled with tears.

As soon as she asked, I produced the small box I had kept hidden in my pocket for the last two days and popped it open, revealing a gold ring with a small heart-shaped diamond.

"Oh, Cecil!"

My voice cracked as I spoke. "Matilda, will you build a life with me? Will you be my wife?" Now, it was my turn for tears.

"Yes—of course, Cecil. Nothing would make me happier."

We rose together, laughter and breath tangled between us, and embraced in joyful disbelief. Beneath the moon's silver light, our shadows merged as we kissed, unrestrained and certain, as though the world itself had narrowed to that single, perfect moment.

As the moment ended, I knew the tricky part was yet to come. I would have to return home and inform my parents that I would not be taking over the family business. I would also not be attending a university for further schooling. Instead, I would move to the Midwest and marry a farmer's daughter. The woman my heart had known I needed, though my mind had not. The details would work themselves out. They would have to. I felt that fate had played a hand in our chance meeting. I was given the opportunity to spread my wings alongside a kindred spirit.

We walked back to the farmhouse hand in hand. Before our engagement could become official, there was one more thing I need to do. I needed to ask permission from my friend John. A knowing look passed between my betrothed and I as we neared the house. "Matilda, could I have a moment with your father?"

Matilda seemed to admire my act of respect. "Why yes, I will be in the kitchen if you need me," she said, slowly letting my hand go as she gracefully walked away. In the doorway, she paused for a moment and looked back at me; her cheeks glowed, and then she stepped through to the kitchen.

To my surprise, nerves it me as I saw John approaching. I allowed myself to calm before I spoke. "Sir, I greatly enjoyed your hospitality and getting to know your family. Especially Matilda. As you may have gathered, Matilda and I have become very close." John's smile widened as if he were able to predict what was coming next. "Would you allow me the pleasure of marrying your daughter?"

"Cecil, my boy, I can't imagine a better match for Matilda." With that, we rejoined the women in the kitchen, both smiling. Matilda had been hiding her hands under her apron up to that point. When she saw us happily returning, she produced her left hand, proudly displaying her ring. Her mother beamed with pride.

Now, all that was left was to go back home and iron out the details with my parents.

# Part 12: Announcing Freedom!

Part 12: Announcing Freedom!

I returned home with a plan. First, I visited the family farm without my father's or mother's knowledge. I presented the gifts I had collected to the family and relayed the details of my adventure, including my engagement to Matilda. Hugs and congratulations were exchanged. The family was thrilled with their gifts, especially my young niece. I kept the visit short, explaining that I must first break the news to my father and mother before I could carry out my plan.

I was going to talk business with my father first, putting him at ease before I announced my own plans. As expected, he jumped at the opportunity to purchase the store in the small town. To my delight He was in a jolly mood and even stated that he was proud of me. I hoped that the mood would soften the blow I was about to deal him.

Now was the time to break the news. I remained calm yet kept a firm tone of voice as I addressed him. "Father, I do not intend to stay here or go to business school. I have no intention of running any of your stores, in fact. I want to move to the Midwest, but not to run a store. I have met someone. We are going to get married and start a farm."

His jaw tensed and twitched a little. Color rose in his face, and a vein began to pulse visibly in his neck. He looked as if his head were about to explode. "That is not your lot in life! You do not get that choice," he growled, stood from his chair, and advanced towards me. He raised his hand as if he were going to strike me. "I will not allow you to regress! I have worked far too hard to build a business to pass on to you and give you a comfortable life! Farming is for simpletons with no education! Not a young man of your social standing!"

I reacted quickly. I had seen this act too many times before. I had had enough. All the years of abuse flowed through my memory as if in slow motion. Each compounded my anger more. Seeing red, I moved towards him, ducking his punch. The old man had slowed with age, and his punch lacked coordination and power. I drew back and threw a right hook with my full body weight behind it. The old man's head snapped sideways, and his face distorted where my fist connected. He staggered back a few steps and fell to the ground with an audible thud. His body fell limp, and his head bounced off the floor twice before resting. There was a look of horror and surprise in his eyes before they rolled back in his head and then closed as he fell unconscious. A trickle of blood dribbled from the corner of his mouth onto the floor beneath him.

I stood, momentarily shocked and surprised by what I had done. It was bound to happen at some point. I had dammed my feelings up for too many years. The dam had finally burst, unleashing my feelings like a raging river. I kneeled next to my father, ensuring he was still breathing. After assuring myself I had not killed him, I stood, relieved.

I knew that this was the beginning of the end of our relationship. I walked towards my mother's bedroom, where I found her sitting in her wheelchair, staring out the window. I knew she had likely heard the altercation.

"Is he dead?" she asked without removing her gaze from the window. I could see from the doorway that her face was drawn with worry.

"No, Mother. I only hit him once. I controlled myself."

With that, she turned her wheelchair to face me. "What was the cause?"

I had dreaded this part of the conversation worse than the part which revealed my plan to my father. I knew this was going to hurt both of us. "Mother, I am not staying. I refuse to be a part of this facade any longer." I started pacing back and forth across the floor. "I will not take over Amos Enterprises. I am choosing the simpler life. I have met someone, and I am going to marry her. We are going to buy land and start our own farm." The words flowed from my mouth so quickly that I was difficult to understand.

My mother was smiling at me, although her face appeared drawn and overly tired. Slow down, Cecil. What happened while you were away?" My mother's voice calmed me. I took a deep breath and took advantage of my father's unconsciousness to explain to my mother, in a very truncated version, what had happened on my business trip.

She waited until I had finished, and then spoke with an authority I had not heard from her in quite some time. "Cecil. I support you. You are right. You are too gentle a soul to stay here and become like your father. You are like your uncles and aunt. I want you to get my nurse from the cottage to tend to him. When he wakes up, I am going to deliver him an ultimatum." Her face seemed to age further as she spoke, knowing what she was doing was releasing me, however, condemning her to life alone with her abuser.

I could not believe the bravery and kindness of this remarkable woman. I went to her, knelt by her side, and gently kissed her cheek. "Mother, why don't you leave him and come with me? I will ensure you are cared for."

My mother raised her chin proudly and looked at me with resolve. "It is too late for me, Cecil. I am old and weakening more by the day. I do not have long left to live on this earth, and I will not burden you."

The selfless words of my mother touched me and gave me further strength to continue. I did not want to leave her here, but her words were clear. Emotions churning within me, I did as she instructed. The wicked old man was still unconscious on the floor. I walked the few feet to the cottage and knocked on the door. When the nurse's husband answered the door, I relayed what had happened. He accompanied his wife to the main house to aid my father as he came to. He sat close by, watching his wife cautiously as she attended to the injured man.

When he came to, he was confused. He touched his face gingerly where my fist had landed. I stood back, watching. He saw me, and the confusion changed to anger. As he tried to stand, the nurse's husband was quickly on his feet, placing a large hand upon my father's shoulder and forcing him back to a seated position. My mother joined us in the room.

"Cedric, for once, you *will* keep quiet and listen to me!" Her voice was commanding.

He started to speak, but quickly stopped when he saw the look given by the Nurse's husband.

"I *have* put up with your abuse. I *have* held my tongue while you slept with other women and even pretended not to notice. I *have* raised our son mostly on my own. And I *have* allowed you your space without saying a word. Now, you *will* allow our son to escape this hell, and you *will* give him the money to do so. If you do not, I *will* no longer be silent. I *will* reveal your secrets to everyone, and then your reputation, along with your precious business, will be ruined." Determination shone in her usually dull eyes as she completed her speech.

My father was flabbergasted by the turn of events. He was physically injured, but his pride was hurt worse. Not since the two were young and dating had my mother shown such passion and spark. I smiled. Now, she and I had been given our chance to show the old man a portion of the pent-up anger we had held in for so long. It was clear that multiple emotions were running through his mind as he sat and glared at the two of us. He seemed to be debating what to do next.

Finally, he spoke. His tone was flat, yet his eyes blazed with anger. He pointed to me, then to my mother. "The two of you may have won this battle, but you will not win the war!" He clenched his fist. "I will give you the money to build your own dream, but first, you will need to get to know that young woman. You will run the store there for one year and court her before I pay for a property and a wedding. If the two of you can make it through a year, then the money will be given to you, and I will ask no more of you."

She and I looked at each other. I tried to decide whether to push back. I felt a tiny flicker of hope. My mother had been waiting for me to say something. I knew that she would fight further if I asked her to. I could see a mix of hope and concern on her drawn, white face. I thought for a moment longer.

"Alright, Father. That is a fair ask. I will give you and this store one more year of my life, but not a moment more. After that year ends, you and Mother must agree to attend Matilda's and my wedding. Mother must remain untouched by your violent hand, or there will be consequences beyond your wildest dreams. Once I have seen the disappointment on your face at seeing me prove you wrong, I want you out of my life." I scowled at him, knowing that he resented the challenge but that he would get no further negotiation from me.

With that, I turned and walked out the door of our family home. I was concerned for my mother, but kept in mind that the hired help was there. I also knew he had taken her threat to heart. This served as further reassurance that he would not renege on our agreement.

I would use my time wisely and further court Matilda. We would make sure it was right for us to be together. Regardless of whether we stayed together or not, I was going to stay in the Midwest and farm as I had dreamed of doing for so long. My father could find someone else to run the business when he became too feeble.

The next day, I sent a telegram to Matilda. I was vague, stating that I would return to the Midwest in another week. I purchased my train ticket, packed everything I owned, and left my room empty. I was heading towards a new chapter in my life and could not have been happier.

# Part 13: Cecil and Matilda

Part 13: Cecil and Matilda

I arrived at Pheasant's Crossing. I had no plan for where to stay, but I knew I would be seeing Matilda, and that was all that mattered. I unloaded all my belongings onto the platform at the train station. To my pleasure, as I hefted the last trunk, Matilda's father, John, stood waiting for me with a warm smile.

"Could you use a hand, Cecil?" he asked with a chuckle.

"John, I was not expecting to see you here." I set the heavy trunk down, breathing a sigh of relief. Sweat ran down my forehead, and I wiped my brow with the back of my shirt sleeve. I offered a handshake but was met with a bear hug from my future father-in-law.

"Matilda was thrilled you were returning. She wanted to greet you herself, but we decided that it would be best if I got you settled first. She will be at our farm waiting for you."

I stood on the platform staring at the older man puzzled. "Get me settled? I have not arranged for lodging yet."

"That is not for you to worry about, son." He scratched at his dark, scruffy beard as he smiled a toothy grin. "We have arranged for you to stay in a cottage on the edge of town. We know the owner and were able to procure it for you as soon as we learned you would be here for good. I brought the truck so we could load your belongings in the bed. I will get you to the new place. It is not fancy, but it will serve as a good roof over your head."

Relief and disbelief washed over me. "John, I do not know how to repay you!"

"Son, you are going to be family. Repayment is not necessary. Frankly, I am glad that you will be nearby. Matilda has been miserable without you."

I took a moment to compose myself before continuing. "Sir, I have some things to discuss with all of you."

"It is late. It can wait until tomorrow. We need to get you to your new home. You can hammer out the details after you have rested. The cottage is fully furnished. We made sure of that, so you won't be sleeping on the floor."

With that, the burly old farmer lofted a trunk with a grunt and headed towards the waiting vehicle. I followed suit. Soon after, we arrived at the cottage on the edge of town. It was a small single-room wooden structure with only the basics. A bed was in one corner, a wood stove in another, used for both heat and cooking, and a few crates converted into shelving and storage. To my delight, there was a sink with working plumbing. It had a small mirror above it and a small shelf beside it. In the center of the room was a square table with four wooden chairs. One corner was sectioned off by a folding divider. There was a small commode behind the wall.

The cottage was small, clean, and had everything I needed. I was not planning on staying past the delegated year, so this would do wonderfully in the meantime. The kindness of my future father-in-law saved me from having to find accommodations on my own.

Soon, all my belongings were moved in. "Thank you, John," I shook his hand. "Have a good night. I will be seeing you tomorrow evening after I take care of business at the store. Promise me, Matilda will be there."

"Oh, I promise. She has been missing you terribly. See you tomorrow, son, and we'll have that discussion you want." He turned away and drove off.

After John had left, I found the trunk containing my toiletries, washed my face, and brushed my teeth before bed. I realized how exhausted I was, yet I felt relieved. I felt... at home. I collapsed on the bed in the corner of my new lodgings and fell into a deep sleep.

I woke up feeling refreshed. I soon realized it was the first time I had slept soundly in so long that I could not recall. This feeling was further proof that I had done the right thing. I was free, or mostly free, of my father and his repression. I knew I had to run the store for a year, but then I could indeed start my life. I rose from my bed, stretched, and yawned. I walked to the small area that served as a kitchen and made myself some coffee. I realized I had not yet brought any food into my new dwelling and made a mental note to do so. I rushed through my morning routine, quickly finding my best suit and slicking my hair back, all in place. I gave myself one last look in the mirror, making sure I looked my best from head to toe.

I left the house and walked to the store with a newfound level of pride in my gait. I waved at familiar folks as I made my way to the store. I arrived at the store and unlocked it with the key given to me. It would be a bit before I could reopen. I wanted to ensure that all the repairs were done and the store was properly stocked before I put the Amos name on the window, leaving in a year or not. After taking careful inventory and making a list of things that needed to be done, I walked back out of the door and locked up. I had no transportation, so I walked to the farm. I removed my coat, threw it over my shoulder, and rolled my sleeves. A slight breeze blew across my face as I started my journey. I took a deep breath, reveling in the fresh air and the fact that I would soon be with my beloved. My spirits continued to lift as I walked to the farm.

As I arrived, I saw Matilda sitting in a wicker chair on the farmhouse's front porch. She observed me quickly approaching. She jumped from her seat and ran towards me, her light blue dress and blonde locks blowing in the wind. It was like a dream. I picked up my pace and ran towards her. We met, and she leaped into my arms. We embraced and kissed with passion. When we finally came back to reality, I saw John and his wife standing on the porch, holding hands and smiling at us. I knew for certain that I had found home.

That afternoon, into the evening, we discussed the details of the arrangement with my father. John looked disgusted as I disclosed those details, along with the upbringing I had endured. Matilda's mother came across the table and wrapped her arms around me. Her family assured me that I would not need to endure my father's abuse any longer. I was accepted by her family. I would finally have a real, loving family with my future wife and her parents. I would have a home built with my own hands.

Fate had finally taken a turn in my favor. After the year I put in under my father's agreement, I would be free to forge the life I truly wanted.

After further discussion, it was decided that Matilda and I would not set a wedding date immediately. We would court first as was proper. We would do our best to learn about each other's traits prior to making the lifelong commitment. We would prove my father wrong. With my new family behind me, I would succeed.

# Part 14: The Dream Begins

Part 14: The Dream Begins

The year passed by in a painfully slow manner. I kept busy. I had the store painted, fixed up, and running to the typical Amos standard. I actually enjoyed running it. We took advantage of the year to learn as much as possible about each other. The more we learned, the more we grew to love each other. I grew to love her family. The challenge my father had thought would break me of the idea of marrying Matilda and starting a life together had brought us closer together. His plan, as I had known it would, backfired.

We set our wedding date for early spring, meeting my father's required time frame. This would allow us to find a plot of land to build on and then get married.

I wired my father with the plans, reminding him of our deal. He agreed to wire the money for our plot of land and a suitable wedding. He also agreed that he and my mother would be present at our wedding. I wrote my dear aunt and uncles, keeping them abreast of my plans. They had been keeping tabs on my parents' home and assured me that Mother was looked after and okay.

The money was received. We began our search for a suitable place to build our future. We agreed that we wanted to remain near Matilda's parents and town, where we could easily retrieve supplies as needed. Matilda's parents were familiar with the area. They knew about the Homestead Act of 1862, which offered free land to anyone over the age of twenty-one who was either single or the head of their household. The only requirement was that the new owner build a dwelling and begin living there within six months. They would also be required to farm at least ten acres of the land. I gladly applied and was fortunate enough to be granted 160 acres.

This would allow me to use all the money I had saved, as well as the money from my father, to build our home and outbuildings, and to buy all the materials needed to build a working farm. Additionally, it would allow me to grant Matilda the wedding of her dreams.

With the help of some of the local farmers I had befriended and John, we picked out a plot of land thirteen miles north of Pheasant's Crossing. It was in an area with rich soil and plentiful water, fed by many underground springs.

The land was flat, with few hills, and virgin ground, just waiting for a plow to break its surface for the first time. The lush prairie grass, appearing as a sea of green, was a good indication that the land would produce well. The lay of the land would allow for a house and outbuildings to be built in the center of our workable land.

The deed to the land was procured in 1925. Matilda wanted a house similar to her parents' home. Together, we would build our dream with the assistance of the community, which had adopted me as one of their own, and the family, who now called me son.

We drew up plans for a story-and-a-half home with four rooms on the main floor and four on the second floor, complete with a cellar. The house and barn were constructed in 1926. The house layout was simple, allowing plenty of room for guests and possibly a family. During the day, I worked on Matilda's parents' farm. I relinquished my cottage on the edge of town in favor of staying in their guest room. I had promised her family that if I were allowed to stay, Matilda and I would be patient and wait. I would make her an honest woman on our wedding night, and not until then.

In the evenings, I, Matilda's father, and whoever else I could get worked on building our little piece of paradise. I cut a driveway in, leading up to the house. I planted lilac bushes around the front of the house to provide shelter from snow and privacy in case the area around us became populated.

As I could afford it, I ensured the house had all the modern conveniences. I hired a professional to install indoor plumbing and ensured the well was deep enough to keep our new home well-supplied with water. I had a large windmill built at the back of the house to pump water into the barn and the house. A large cistern was also dug and lined with concrete for additional water storage.

As per Matilda's request, the kitchen was one of the largest rooms on the main floor. The large wood stove sat in one corner. Oak cabinets with polished granite countertops lined three sides of the room, along with large storage cabinets above them. One large floor-to-ceiling cabinet was built as a pantry. A large porcelain sink was installed in the center of the largest countertop, directly under a window overlooking the side yard. I could picture Matilda standing by the sink, working on canning fresh food or making a meal to be enjoyed by our future children. The thought warmed my heart.

The other three rooms were a sitting-dining room combination, a master bedroom, and a real bathroom with plumbing. The floors were made of maple and polished to a sheen. The upper level of the house was left mainly as a blank canvas. I imagined it would have our bedroom, and the rest would be for guests. I hoped we would one day fill the additional rooms with children.

I built a large porch in the back of the house. I imagined sitting on the porch in a rocking chair, watching the sunrise, and sitting with Matilda. The possibilities created by this new home were immeasurable. The new house's exterior was painted white, with black shutters around each window. The black asphalt shingles matched the shutters. I left room on both sides of the house for the flower beds, which Matilda had also requested.

The large barn was placed north of the house, leaving ample pasture for the animals. The barn was standard. It included a lean-to that was open and had a dirt floor. There was a door the size of a standard entry door, but split into two sections, leading into the main portion of the barn to the right. Entry to the next room required both door sections to be opened. The main portion of the barn was split up into three sections. A half wall separated the sections. I built sturdy wooden gates running vertically, creating two large stalls and a large open area. I imagined horses, cows, and maybe a couple of goats in the barn.

The third section was a smaller room with its own door. It had a hydrant and a couple of shelves built into the walls. This area would be used to store feed for our animals and keep equipment organized.

A set of steps led up to the hay loft. The stairs were built to be sturdy and support the weight of whatever needed to be hauled. The hay loft itself was open. I knew that this was where we would hold our wedding. After the wedding, it would serve as a place to store straw and hay for our animals. We would need to add additional outbuildings for crop storage, a chicken coop, and maybe an area for equipment storage.

As the farm neared completion, Matilda and I began planning our wedding. We invited all our friends and family, and we would hold the wedding dance and the reception in our barn.

What we presumed was an early wedding present arrived just before the wedding date. It was delivered in a large wooden crate made of pine slats, about 5.5 feet tall and 6 feet wide. It was clearly cumbersome, as several people were needed to unload it into our yard. There had been no warning, and we had no idea what could be in the large wooden crate with our names and the names of Matilda's parents printed in red block letters.

We decided to open the box rather than wait until the wedding. After all, it must have been meant to be opened since it had arrived early. Matilda could not hide her excitement. I followed behind her, grinning, as she skipped to the newly built barn and began rooting around in the tack room, looking for tools. I joined her search. Eventually, she found a hammer, and I found a crowbar.

"Alright, we found the tools! Now, let's pry this big box open and see what kind of surprise my parents have in store for us! I can only imagine what it could be," she squealed with excitement. "Do you think it's alive?"

At the remark, I burst into laughter. "Matilda, there is no way anything could possibly be alive in a box like that."

Matilda looked at me, trying not to laugh, but she could not hold back. Now, we were both laughing. Had anyone seen us at that moment, holding tools and laughing until tears rolled from our eyes, they would have thought us to be children. Not young adults about to get married. Moments like this further assured me that joining our lives permanently was the right decision. How could anything that felt so right ever go wrong?

We held hands as we returned to the crate that sat near the newly built house. "Well, dear, do you want to start, or should I?" I asked as I rested the hammer on my shoulder.

With that, Matilda thrust the claw end of the pry bar into a crack of the crate, hoping to find some purchase on the wood, enabling her to pry off a board. I watched as the delicate yet sturdy woman's face reddened as she struggled to free whatever may lie inside the crate.

"Let me try, dear," I said cautiously, careful not to suggest that she was lacking. She had worked just as tirelessly as I had to complete our home. She was strong and determined, merely unfamiliar with the tools. Still, she always tried, and with each task she took on, I could see her growing more confident and skilled.

She handed over the pry bar with a pouty look, "Fine."

"It is all right, dear. You can help. Just let me see if I can get some of these boards loose. I promise you can be the one to open it once I get it started." I smiled gently to reassure my future wife. I loosened all the slats on top, then one side of the crate, and handed the hammer back to Matilda. "Are you ready, dear?" I asked with a smile.

She squealed with excitement as she took the hammer from me. "Thank you, Cecil," she said in her sweet, melodious voice. She placed a kiss on the tip of my nose, one of those things that some would find odd but had become a special gesture of affection between the two of us. Then she set to work. The rough wooden handle of the claw hammer contrasted with her smooth, milky white skin as she gripped it tightly with both hands. She stood on her tiptoes, pried off the top planks of the crate, and then removed the front planks, leaving only three sides and the bottom. As she did, the gift became visible.

To both of our surprise, it was a brand-new player piano! We both stared at the polished mahogany body and the bright white ivory keys with black centers. "Oh my Goodness! It's too much," Matilda whispered in awe.

I was speechless. My thoughts raced through where the gift might belong and the many purposes it could serve. Since it had been given to celebrate our union, it felt only right that its first use be saved for the ceremony itself. It would provide the perfect music for both the vows and the barn dance that followed. Leave it to Matilda's wonderful, wise parents to recognize what we had been missing. It would take some effort, but together we devised a plan to hire several strong men to haul it up into the loft.

As we stood looking as our gift, relief washed over me. I realized the piano was the final piece of the puzzle. The plans were set, and our home was built. The only thing left were the finishing touches. Now it was time to take a break.

Matilda and I retired to the back porch to sit rocking in our matching wicker rocking chairs. It was only weeks before our wedding date. She sighed softly and reached over, her delicate hand settling into my rough, weathered palm. I looked down and smiled, seeing the noticeable difference. Her hands had begun to gain a slightly rough texture while helping to build our home. Dreams of the future danced through both of our heads. "There is still something missing, Cecil," Matilda stated.

I tilted my head towards her and stopped rocking. "What are you thinking about, my love?"

She stopped rocking as well and squinted her eyes. She lifted her other hand and pointed to the south side of our house. "I would like a fruit orchard. I could care for it, and it would provide us with a variety of food, as well as preserves that I could sell. It is something I could call my own."

I looked at her curiously. "My dear, where has this idea come from? You do remember how cold winters get here, don't you?"

"Cecil, do you think me daft?" Matilda's thoughtful squint quickly turned to a pout. She stood up and walked purposefully into our home. The quick change in mood left me reeling. I wondered what she could possibly be going after, as we had firmly committed to not cohabitating until after we had married.

Matilda halted in the living area, beside a box still packed with belongings awaiting their proper place. She dug through its contents momentarily. "Here, take a look. I found this book amongst your belongings at Mother and Father's house." Matilda opened the thick, hard-covered book. It contained yellowed pages with text and illustrations. She turned to a page she had marked with a bookmark she had braided out of thick pink yarn.

I took the book, looking at the page she had marked. Matilda had underlined several paragraphs, each with a picture of a tree drawn by the author. Each page contained specifics about variations of fruit trees, including the height and approximate width of each tree when grown, what the leaves and flowers looked like, and the climate in which each could be grown. The trees Matilda had selected were a self-pollinating pear, several apple varieties, apricot trees, and plum trees all other than the pear would require multiple trees to produce fruit. I looked at my fiancée with newfound respect in my eyes. "My love, you have done your research! This may be something to consider. However, we must first purchase the necessities."

Matilda seemed a bit disappointed but did not argue. Little did she know that with the newfound knowledge she had just revealed, I was planning a wedding surprise of my own. I would only need to find out where I could procure some of these treasures.

The next day, I left alone, using the excuse of needing supplies for her father's farm. Instead of going to town, I drove a bit further to a neighboring town with a university. I discovered that the Agriculture Department was researching the viability of the same trees that the beautiful love of my life was interested in. I discussed the possibility of the University allowing us to assist in their research by planting some of the trees at our farm. Terms were agreed upon because, as luck had it, the University was seeking land to plant specimens for student study. I decided we would allow students to visit our land. However, my fiancée was to be the primary caretaker, and we were to be able to raise the trees and sell or use the fruit as we saw fit. I was excited to share the wedding present with Matilda. The best part was that the University would benefit from using our land at no cost. I arranged for the trees to be delivered a week before our wedding. We would use five acres to the south of our house for the fruit orchard.

Knowing how much Matilda loved color, I ordered several beautiful species of flowers from the university as an additional present. Not only would she have the trees she wanted, but she could fill her flower beds. I left the meeting feeling quite satisfied with myself. Keeping the secret was challenging, but the result was worth it. The wedding would be in two weeks, after all. My only concern was ensuring the trees were in place beforehand.

The trip, which I had initially thought would be short, had ended up taking a majority of the day. Discussing what was needed, and finding terms with the college had been a lengthy process. I returned home that evening, exhausted. I knew I would need some assistance, if I were going to pull the surprise off. Matilda was nowhere to be found to my pleasure. In fact the house appeared to be empty, with only the scent of supper indicating that the family was near-by. I searched around outside and found John working on a piece of machinery. He stopped what he was doing upon my approach. "Good evening, Cecil! Looks like you have been a busy man," he replied in his always upbeat tone.

"Yes, sir. I have something I need to share with you if you have a bit." With that, he stopped his work completely, and gave me his full attention. I shared in detail what I had actually been up to during the day. Another way to ensure the happiness of his daughter in her new home. He was very pleased. He agreed to help with planting the trees, bushes, and flowers as time allowed him. As it turned out, he was as eager to ensure the happiness of our union as I was. He offered to involve Mildred in the placement, ensuring a woman's touch was felt.

Both John and I left the discussion with a feeling of accomplishment. I was very quiet during our family meal. I explained my exhaustion to Matilda and Mildred with made-up details about my day and how busy it had been. John quietly smiled from the head of the table. I excused myself, kissed Matilda on the cheek, and retired to my quarters for some much-needed sleep. That night, I had the loveliest dream I could ever remember in my adult life.

In the dream, the farm appeared complete. The beautiful white house with new shingles and black shutters was lit up inside. Matilda stood at the sink, smiling as she washed dishes.

The house was bordered on two sides by perfectly manicured flower beds. Suddenly, Matilda was present again as if by magic. This time, she was outside, near the house, picking a plump pink peony from the luscious green bush. A small flock of chickens and a couple of ducks plucked at the short grass on the ground nearby. Matilda lifted the flower to her nose and smiled delicately as its sweet fragrance entered her nostrils.

The house had a porch at both the front and the back. I watched, as though from a distance, an image of the two of us seated together on the back porch, rocking gently in unison. We faced the sunset, its pinks, oranges, and golds washing over a hedge of lilac bushes along the western edge of the property, their pale purple buds glowing softly in the fading light. To the south, there was the grove of fruit trees. These were in full bloom. All the varieties that I had seen in the textbook were present and fully grown. They looked healthy, and it appeared it would be a plentiful harvest.

To the east of the house was a larger fruit tree. It appeared to be several trees grown together, as indicated by the twisted look of its trunk. I could not tell what type of tree this was. Matilda was near it, fretting over the base of its trunk, ensuring no overgrown grass or foliage was near it. It appeared to be a favorite of hers. Fields with newly sprouting crops bordered three sides of the property.

Beyond the fourth edge of the property stretched a wide pasture, dotted with cattle, horses, and goats grazing behind the great barn we had only just finished raising. Two smaller outbuildings stood apart from it—one for the goats, the other a simple lean-to offering shelter to the cattle. The animals appeared well fed and content, moving with the easy rhythm of a life undisturbed. If this were the future set before us, it promised long, quiet years upon our small patch of paradise, so peaceful it felt almost unreal.

# Part 15: Wedding Day

Part 15: Wedding Day

Excitement filled the air on May 1, 1926, was the day of our wedding. Spring had come early, and the air was already warm. The fruit trees had taken root, among them a peculiar pear tree—one that already bore the unmistakable shape of several trunks twisted together into a single form. Though it was still young and unbloomed, the sight of it stirred something deep within me, an image half-remembered of what it would one day become, tall and heavy with fruit. Matilda had insisted on planting this tree herself and tending it alone. For now, its branches were thick with lush green leaves, full of promise, as though quietly reaching toward a future I felt I had seen before.

The yard around the house and leading up to the barn was neatly mowed. The newly obtained small herd of Black Angus cattle, four Quarter Horses, two black, a bay, and a buckskin, and two goats grazed in the pasture. The animals had not yet been allowed into the barn, so it could remain in pristine condition for the wedding. The player piano had been placed in the rear of the hayloft to prevent it from taking up space that would be needed for feed storage once the wedding was over. Friends and family had decorated the hayloft, and we had not been allowed to see it.

Matilda and I had carefully chosen our wedding colors to complement our best features: my dark hair and blue eyes, and Matilda's beautiful blonde locks. We wanted to look our best on our special day.

I had been allowed to see Matilda's dress after its completion, but would not be allowed to see it on my beautiful fiancée until the day of our wedding. Matilda chose a traditional white as the main color of her dress. It was eloquent with Edwardian-style flowing lines. The bodice was fit to accent her ample bosom. The waistline hugged just above her hips, revealing her feminine curves. The fabric was silk, with blue and gray lace accents on the bodice, sleeves, and bottom. Matilda chose a traditional white lace veil with simple blue accents along the hems, matching her dress. As it was of her own design, it was one of a kind. Dancing and singing were two of her favorite pastimes. She chose to have her dress hemmed at the ankles to allow her to move with ease and to ensure she could enjoy the wedding dance afterward. Her shoes were simple, flat dress shoes, further allowing for comfort during the wedding and dance.

I purchased a thick silver chain bearing a single round pendant and two diamond-shaped pendants set with turquoise, meant to rest at the gentle V of her neckline. I chose a matching silver bracelet and a pair of diamond-shaped silver earrings with turquoise inlays, imagining how they would catch the light when she moved. When I gave them to her, her delight was immediate and unguarded, and it warmed me more than I had expected. In that moment, I felt certain that we had truly come to know one another, our shared time shaping not only affection, but an understanding of the smallest, most personal tastes.

I took equal care with my own appearance, wanting to stand before her as the man she had chosen. I wore a new white suit coat with matching trousers, tailored to fit me as though made with her eyes in mind. Beneath it, a light blue button-down shirt framed my shoulders and chest, its color chosen not by chance but for how it complemented me. At my throat, I fastened a bolo tie—silver and diamond-shaped, set with turquoise—then completed the look with a gray cowboy hat and well-polished boots. The blue of my shirt and the stone at my neck drew out the color of my eyes, setting them bright against the white cloth and dark hair. I hoped that when she looked at me, she would see not the clothes, but the care behind them—and know they were worn for her alone.

As I did not have siblings, I called upon my two uncles to be my groomsmen. They were thrilled to be a part of my day, as they had been so much a part of my decision to form this new life I had grown to love. My closest friend Elliott, whom I had met at the local tavern and quickly befriended upon my move to Pheasant's Crossing, was to stand up for me. Elliott had been of great help in learning what would be required to start a successful farm in the area. He quickly became my closest confidant, and I knew he was the only choice. He quickly agreed. Each wedding party member visited a tailor and purchased a fitted black suit coat and trousers, along with a matching light blue shirt.

With no relatives living nearby, Matilda chose three of her closest friends from town to stand beside her. Her family was well known and warmly regarded in the community, and she had many friends to choose from, selecting only those dearest to her to share in the day. She planned every detail alongside her best friend, Lila, whose happiness at being included matched her own.

With their family farms so close, the two spoke often, their conversations filled with anticipation and laughter. Laura, who had once worked briefly in my store, and Barbara—whose beauty was the envy of many in Pheasant's Crossing—completed the group. Together, the four were among the loveliest women in the area, and Matilda, the last of them to marry, seemed to glow with the knowledge. Each bridesmaid wore a light blue silk dress trimmed with gray lace, the final touch in a celebration already alive with excitement.

On the day of the wedding, the yard quickly filled with automobiles. It would have appeared to the outside world that all of Pheasant's Crossing was present. The mood was jovial amongst the guests, all except my father and mother. Their expensive attire stood out among the crowd of farmers and local merchants, more closely resembling that of the bride and groom.

My parents' arrival was unlike that of any other guest, impossible to ignore even as I moved through the crowd with my groomsmen. My father passed among the well-wishers with practiced indifference, acknowledging no one—not even his own brothers and sister. He propelled my mother forward as though she were an inconvenience rather than a partner, and when they reached the stairway to the loft, he wordlessly lifted her from her chair and carried her upward. They took their seats at the front, silent and rigid, a chill seeming to settle around them. My father stared straight ahead, unmoving. My mother sat dutifully at his side, pale and unnaturally thin, her eyes flicking toward him with quiet hope, only to fall again when no attention was returned.

I remained where I was, smiling, shaking hands, speaking pleasantries as though my chest were not tightening with every step they took. From my place in the crowd, I watched the other guests part for them, watched curiosity give way to discomfort as guests realized no introductions would be offered. No one there had ever met my parents. I caught sight of my future father-in-law, arms crossed, his expression dark with immediate understanding. When our eyes met, I knew he recognized exactly who had arrived. He started toward them, broad shoulders set, but I quickly signaled for him to stop. He hesitated, then nodded, though the caution in his gaze remained. I returned to my role as host, my voice steady, my laughter practiced—determined that no one would see how deeply their presence had unsettled me.

I quickly ended the conversation I had been participating in, shaking the hand of the Mayor politely and making my way towards the barn. The moment of confrontation I had been avoiding since I had last left home was upon me. I needed to speak with my father. My mother's worsening frailty had not escaped my attention. I could feel my face reddening as I neared the top of the stairs leading to the loft. I stopped where I was not visible, closed my eyes, and took a deep breath. This was my wedding day. I was not going to let the cruel man who had ruined my youth ruin my wedding day. I felt my blood pressure and heart rate return to normal as I schooled my face. I allowed myself to take in the beauty of the decorations our wedding party had so carefully placed, which further lightened my mood.

I knew that the silent couple had heard my approach, as the click of my boot heels on the wooden floor seemed amplified by the silence in the loft. My mother turned to face me, smiling. I watched as my father silently grasped her wrist, and the smile dropped from her face. I had to fight the urge to react to his cruelty.

"Father, Mother, you have made it!" I exclaimed with as much joy as I could muster from my voice. "I am so happy to see you." I pasted a smile on my clean-shaven face, allowing my straight white teeth to show through my thin-lipped smile.

Finally, my father rose. "Cecil, as per our arrangement, I am here," he said in a cold, flat tone. His hair had thinned, and he was now slightly stooped. His heavily lined face remained unsmiling. His aged appearance surprised me.

I was met with only one hand outstretched as if to shake the hand of an acquaintance. At this, my smile dropped. I knew, undoubtedly, that this relationship was not to be mended. His cold attitude showed me that this may very well be the last dealing I had with the weathered, cruel, old businessman. I was no longer his beloved son, heir to the Amos fortune. I would be on my own to forge my future.

I shook his hand with a powerful grip. I hoped the grip implied my confidence and showed the old man that I was not afraid to move forward without him. I shot him a steely glare and quickly moved to my mother. I scooped her frail body off the seat into my burly arms. She squealed in delight at my gentle yet strong embrace. I placed a soft kiss upon her bony white cheek. "Mother, it has been far too long!"

Her voice had weakened. I looked at her carefully as I held her in my arms and realized how sad her eyes looked despite the smile on her face. She weighed close to nothing. Her disability had taken all the muscles from her legs. Her face was drawn and filled with even more lines than my father's. She reminded me of a small child despite her aged appearance. Fragile and innocent.

My mother leaned close, her breath trembling against my ear, careful to keep her voice low so my father would not notice. "Cecil, my dear, sweet son—how I have missed you." Her words rushed together, as though time itself were slipping from her grasp. "I must speak quickly. We have so little time before your father intervenes. My health is failing faster now, and I know, in my heart, that this will be the last time I see you." She pressed her cheek briefly against mine, so light it was almost a memory. "I love you more than I can ever say. Remember that I will always be with you, watching over you. I want nothing for you but happiness—with your beautiful wife and the life you are beginning today." She drew back, forcing a small, brave smile. "Now, please—put me down and go on with your duties, before he notices."

A small tear ran down her cheek as she wheezed a bit before coughing. I leaned my head down to her shoulder and snuggled against her as I had done so many times as a young child. A tear escaped my eye, but I knew I could not let my father see the emotion. I inhaled the scent of lavender and vanilla, which would forever remind me of my mother, closed my eyes tightly for a moment, and then quickly composed myself before placing her back in her seat. Raising my gaze to meet that of my father's once again, I concentrated on Matilda and I's upcoming union instead of thinking further about my mother's state. He stood nearby with his arms crossed, looking as if he wanted to say something.

"I love you both," I said, preparing to rejoin the wedding guests. I gazed directly into my mother's eyes as I did. I pulled my silver pocket watch from the pocket of my trousers and glanced. The wedding was quickly approaching, and it was time to find the wedding party and let the ushers guide our guests to their seats.

Mixed emotions filled my chest a I looked around at the yellow bales of straw arranged in rows along the walls for seating, and the chairs placed at the front of the seating area for older people. I observed the blue and gray cray paper decorating the rafters, the walls, and the banner near the rear of the loft over the podium set up for the preacher.

My parents looked small, sitting there alone. For a moment, I felt guilty about leaving them to fend for themselves. In truth, it was my mother whom I felt sorry for. I felt nothing but contempt for the wicked man next to her. With that, I went back to the crowd without any further words.

The rest of the day felt like a beautiful, perfect dream. The music flowed melodiously from the player piano as the internal reel spun round and round. The keys moved magically on their own. The loft was at full capacity. Not a single seat to spare. My groomsmen ascended the stairs to the loft single file. I followed. "It is time," Elliot whispered as he slapped me on the back. I grinned wordlessly as I began my ascent upward to my waiting future.

We lined up on the left side of the altar, where the preacher stood, smiling, Bible open, ready to unite Matilda and me in marriage before God and our families. Next, I watched eagerly as the bride's maids came to stand at the right of the altar. After the entire wedding party was in place, the piano music was changed. I took a deep breath, attempting to ground myself. This was it. This was her queue. Excitement and expectation filled the room as the crowd of guests went silent and rose to their feet.

"Here Comes the Bride" began playing note by note. I stood, waiting. The suspense was the worst I have ever felt. Time seemed to slow to a crawl as I looked towards the staircase. As if by magic, she appeared. Her father held her arm securely as they walked towards me. The rest of the room seemed to disappear. My vision held only Matilda, in a white, flowing dress, walking slowly towards me. She walked towards our future together, one step at a time. John deposited his daughter beside me in front of the preacher. Tears of happiness streamed down the mighty man's face as he kissed his beloved daughter on the cheek and then nodded to me before being seated next to Midred. Matilda now stood across from me. She gazed in my direction, tears of joy threatening to spill from her beautiful eyes at any moment.

The moment we had both been waiting for was here. The pastor began the ceremony. "Dearly Beloved..." The ceremony flew by. I have no recollection of it. "I now pronounce you man and wife. You may kiss the bride," our pastor announced, his pride and happiness apparent in his voice. These words snapped me back to reality. I turned to my new bride, smiling as wide as I could. I joined hands with Matilda with my right hand, placed my left hand on her face, and drew her to me. We kissed a long, gentle kiss. The first of what I hoped would be many to come as a married couple. The crowd cheered. The wait was over! We were now man and wife. It was time to celebrate!

The piano played a rousting melody as we exited the loft for a few minutes of privacy before the reception and dance. Matilda and I took the opportunity to enter our house as newlyweds for the first time. We crossed the front porch hand in hand. As we approached the door of our new home, I abruptly stopped, sweeping my new wife into my arms and carrying her across the threshold into our house. Matilda giggled as I did so. I had never been happier.

"Cecil, put me down," she squeaked between giggles. "I want us to walk through the house together before we go back for our reception."

"Your wish is my command, my love," I said as I stood her back on her feet. Now, it was my turn to giggle.

We crossed the threshold together, and suddenly every room felt too small to contain us. Our footsteps echoed as we wandered from space to space, laughing at nothing in particular, pausing to take in corners we already knew by heart. The house seemed to breathe around us, warmed by lamplight and the hum of shared anticipation.

Matilda drifted to the sink and rested her hands on the sill, gazing out at the neat rows of newly planted fruit trees. She shook her head, a quiet laugh escaping her. "I still can't believe you made this happen." When she turned to me, her eyes were bright with something deeper than pride. "Soon we'll plant the crops, bring in the animals. We'll build a life here—a business and a home."

We collapsed onto the red velvet couch, sinking into its softness as though it had been waiting for us alone, our shoulders brushing as we admired the stone-faced fireplace. Passing through the dining room, I trailed my hand along the smooth surface of the handcrafted table, wide enough to seat six. "We'll either need to invite plenty of friends and family," I said, wagging my eyebrows, "or start filling it ourselves."

Matilda's answering smile was all mischief and promise.

We slowly went upstairs to our bedroom, stood at the doorway, and looked at the large four-post bed. No words were said. Only an anxious smile was exchanged between the two of us. As if reading each other's thoughts, we walked through the rest of the upper level of the house.

"We should probably return to our guests, Mr. Amos," Matilda stated.

"Why, yes, I believe the time has come, Mrs. Amos." The words flowed smoothly off my tongue.

"I love you, Mr. Amos," she said as we joined hands and returned to our guests.

The scene in the barn had changed in the short period we had been gone. The doors to the front of the barn were opened. The lean-to area now contained tables and chairs. The crowd had grown. There was a large table in the center, covered with what looked like a feast, and guests were surrounding it, patiently awaiting our return. At the head of the table was Mildred, who was now wearing an apron over her light blue dress. Upon seeing us, she smiled broadly, grabbing a piece of silverware from the table and chinking it against the glass punch bowl filled with a red liquid.

"May I have your attention, please?" she belted out. "The newlywed Mr. and Mrs. Cecil Amos have entered the building."

Matilda turned red at the attention we were receiving. I placed one arm around her protectively and raised the other, waving to the crowd.

My mother had wheeled herself to the other end of the table. Some of the color had returned to her face, and she was smiling. It appeared that she and Matilda's mother had become friends. My father stood at the far side of the crowd, away from everyone else, a sour look on his face and his arms crossed firmly over his chest.

Matilda's father joined the group at the head table, his usual friendly smile larger than normal. "Cecil, would you like to say a few words and then say the prayer before we eat?"

I nodded in response, placing an arm around my new wife's waist. I took a few steps in the direction of the table, leading and overwhelmed Matilda through the crowd. "Thank you all for joining us today. In the short time I have lived in Pheasant's Crossing, it has become home. I want to thank each of you for making me welcome." I shot a glance at my father as I continued. "John and Mildred, I would like to extend special thanks to you for welcoming me into your family and allowing me the honor of courting your daughter, working for you during that time, the time it took to build our home, and most importantly, allowing me to take her hand in marriage."

As I finished my speech, John approached me and clasped a large hand on my shoulder. My father's glare became more noticeable as he stared at me across the room. It felt as if he were trying to start me on fire.

Now, it was Matilda's turn to speak. She grasped my hand as if looking for encouragement. I gave her hand a light squeeze. She cleared her throat. "Thank you, friends and family. Your support is something I cannot express my gratitude for in enough words. With your continued support, Cecil and I hope to make a valuable contribution to the community through the business we will build." As she spoke, her voice grew in confidence. I could feel her love and gratitude passing between our connected hands.

I waited a moment after she had finished, gazing at her with nothing less than total adoration. Then, I closed my eyes as I said my prayer, "Father God, I want to thank You for today. I want to thank You for our friends and family making the safe trip to us, for the food before us, and for the fellowship here today. Most of all, thank You for the beautiful woman I have taken today as my wife. We humbly ask for your blessing upon our union, for our future success in our business, and for a long and happy marriage. Amen."

With that, John's voice erupted from the silence as he happily announced, "Let's eat!" We were served first, along with the wedding party. The table contained beef, pork, and chicken. There were multiple types of salads. In the center was a large three-tier wedding cake with blue and gray accents and small figures resembling Matilda and me on top. Matilda's mother served each person with assistance from my mother as they passed. I was concerned that Mother might overexert herself, so I kept a close eye on her. Her face contained an energy I had not seen in quite some time. She looked happy.

All enjoyed the meal. There were interruptions for speeches from my Best Man and Matilde's Maid of Honor. The parents declined to speak. There were laughs, and silverware clinked on glass many times, signaling that we should kiss. We gladly accepted each time, unable to get enough of each other. Finally, it was time to cut the cake.

Matilda and I eagerly approached the main table, removed the figures from the top of the cake, and then joined hands on the knife to cut the tiers together. We cut each tier into small pieces and finally, each grabbed a small square piece. We crossed arms, each holding a piece in the opposite hand of the other. We lifted the pieces to each other's mouths. As if on cue, Matilda's face turned mischievous. Her piece of cake promptly smashed gently into my nose. I looked at her in surprise and gasped, my mouth forming an O. I brought my hand to my face, wiping the white frosting from my nose. I cocked my head and promptly wiped the frosting onto her nose. We were laughing uncontrollably now, and the crowd joined. Finally, we took a bite of each other's cake. Then, the guests were allowed to partake.

After everyone had a chance to eat and visit, we filed back to the barn's loft. The benches were gone, and only the player piano and some rows of bales for seating remained. John, switched the piano rolls as needed since he had given the gift. Once everyone had returned to the loft, he announced our first dance as husband and wife.

"Ladies and Gentlemen, let's welcome the new Mr. and Mrs. Amos to the dance floor for their first dance!"

We made our way to the center of the floor, where a spotlight shone. The first few notes of a slow love song drifted from the piano, and Mildred sang along to the familiar tune in a soft, sweet voice. I closed my eyes, entirely content, as Matilda and I leaned into one another, joined as husband and wife. Happiness radiated through my entire body; my eyes sparkled with adoration, and my sharp features softened with love.

# Part 16: Building the Farm

Part 16: Building the Farm

After the wedding, Matilda and I settled into a comfortable routine. We both worked very hard. Matilda tended the trees, ensuring they had water and the proper fertilizer so they would be well-established before the first frost. We knew that they would not produce for the first few years, so the payoff would be a while in the future. I enjoyed watching her tend to each tree. Her care in the project was visible. She paid particular attention to the pear tree she had planted. It had begun to look even more twisted. I suggested we try to untwist what appeared to have been multiple trees. She refused this idea, stating that she liked it as it was. The trunks growing together reminded her of us growing close together as a couple. I enjoyed her analogy, and her happiness mattered to me.

While tractors, reapers, and threshers were becoming popular, I kept our costs low and stuck with basic farm equipment. I purchased a horse-drawn plow. My other tools were mostly hand tools. I had not planned to reap a crop during our first year, but I had determined to get the acres we wanted to farm plowed. Plans changed as we were progressing much more quickly than expected with our work. As I finished the plowing, we made a decision. We decided we would; indeed do at least some planting during our first year on our new place. I only planted a small portion of the land at first because the season started late. I knew from studying some of Matilda's books that the corn would need to be planted by mid-June at the very latest and the beans a bit earlier. I would also plant some winter wheat closer to fall to have two separate harvests.

Even once we were planting everything we intended during the following year, we would keep a portion of our land as pasture for our growing herd. We added several Holsteins to our menagerie. Throughout winter, we would be able to sell some of the milk from them and ensure we had enough to keep for ourselves. Their milk along with what we grew, eggs from the chickens and me at from the animals kept for that purpose would keep us well supplied without having to buy much in town.

I was thankful for my business background, though I resented being forced into it. I was even more grateful to my aunt and uncles for teaching me how to make a farm work. I knew this first year would be challenging, but I had confidence that it could only get better moving forward as long as we were willing to do the work. There was nothing that my new wife and I could not accomplish together.

During the following month, we continued to work tirelessly: I plowed and planted, and Matilda worked in the house, helped care for our animals, and maintained the fruit grove.

The days were all similar, and began to blur together as we worked towards our common goal. They always started with Matilda up before me, preparing breakfast for us and coffee to go in my thermos. We ate together and I kissed her, even if it was just a short peck, before I headed out to work in the fields for the day. I was always provided with lunch to take with me, so I would never go hungry while working. My appreciation for my wife grew by the day.

The only exception was Sunday. That day was set aside as a day of rest, and worship. Only the necessary maintenance of our animals was completed, as well as meals for ourselves.

At first, the days were spent plowing. It was exhausting, back breaking work that left me no energy for anything else. It became more and more noticeable that the work was going to be too much for both myself and my animals. After discussing my dilemma with Matilda, I added a team of Draft Horses to our stable. The Quarter Horses were simply not enough for the number of acres that needed to be worked. This eased the burden on my horses, but not on me. Further discussion was had with Matilda. There were only three choices. To ask her help in the field along with everting else she was already doing, continue to try to keep up on my own, or to hire someone to help.

The first two options were simply not practical. I hired a man to assist with the work. Harold was a very tall man with huge, calloused hands, broad shoulders, and a slight pot belly. He was constantly dirty, and one did not dare get too close to him due to his noticeably offensive body odor. His brown hair was always greasy, and his teeth were yellowed and decaying. Upon his arrival, he only had one set of clothing: a brown button-down shirt and a tattered pair of overalls, which he rarely washed. His boots were well-worn, with holes in the soles.

He was not much of a speaker. He had a speech impediment that kept him from communicating clearly. He was, however, a very hard worker. He did not ask for any money for his efforts, only a roof over his head and food in his belly. I was quick to hire him.

Matilda, ever the compassionate one, noticed his plight. She quickly requested that we buy him some new clothing, give him access to indoor plumbing, and provide him with a room and food. I studied the man, considering whether he would be worth the additional expense. I looked deeply into his eyes, seeing nothing but honesty. The following day, we went into town and bought him several sets of clothing, including some dress clothes, two new pairs of boots, and a hat to keep the sun out of his eyes as he worked.

Harold was overjoyed to possess more than he had ever had in his life. In return for our kindness, he worked hard for us. He quickly became a trusted friend and an invaluable help around the farm. Living under the same roof as him, we quickly learned to decipher what he was communicating. He reluctantly told us his story around the dinner table one evening. When Harold was young, he suffered a serious injury after falling from the second story of a barn he was helping to build. The fall left him unconscious for days, and though his body healed, the damage to his head did not fully mend. From that day forward, his speech was slow and halting, each word shaped by the injury he carried with him—a lasting reminder of how quickly a single moment could alter a life. Since then, no one, including his family, had accepted him. We shared our home with him and welcomed him as family. I would not have completed the tasks I needed in my first year without his help. He would become even more important at the end of our story, but we had no way of knowing at the time.

Though Harold's help made the days a bit shorter, the work still required us toiling from sunup through sundown. During the next month, we did the impossible. We plowed all the planned land and planted corn and beans in the fields. We were exhausted by the end of June, but the sense of accomplishment was well worth it. We knew that, barring any natural disaster, we would have a crop sometime between August and October. The beans would be ripe between October and November. We would begin planting winter wheat around the middle of harvest. All we could do was wait and hope that winter would come late, allowing us to complete the required work to carry us into the following year. The beans would be harvested and sold, hopefully at a profit. Part of the corn would be kept to feed our animals. The stalks would be harvested as supplemental feed during the winter months when the animals could not graze outside.

The ever helpful Matilda had grown a large garden full of vegetables. There were rows of sweet corn, carrots, peas, tomatoes, peppers, onions, potatoes, squash, and cucumbers. There were also rows of herbs, including dill, garlic, basil, thyme, lavender, and mint. These crops were to be canned or dried at the end of the season. They would be stored in the cellar below the house and rationed throughout the winter, when they were needed most. Some would be consumed fresh as a treat with the meals as they ripened.

Matilda was an excellent cook, having learned from her mother. She proved to be an even harder worker than I had ever thought. My appreciation for her grew beyond what I had thought possible. The house was always clean, the dishes done, meals made, and she maintained the orchard and garden on her own. She also helped with the fields as best she could when she could and cared for the animals once a day. Though our time together was sparse, and most new wives would have complained, she never did. She dutifully completed her chores without complaint and always greeted me with a smile. Her hard work and bright attitude did not go unnoticed. I knew that I was neglecting my new wife. I knew I needed to find a way to show her. My biggest fear was that she would feel unfulfilled and leave me. After all, we had barely had a chance to try for the family she wanted, with all the work that came with our new home.

That first spring and summer on the farm were more difficult than I could have ever imagined. There was no rest nor an end in sight. We all survived.

Luck had smiled upon us with perfect weather. Just the right amount of rain had fallen, and there had been no severe storms. The corn had grown tall and straight with thick cobs of gold attached to the slowly ripening stalks. It looked like we would have plenty to sell and feed our herd. The beans had ripened to the color of straw, with pods full and bursting. All our heifers had been bred to our bull, with timing that should work out well with planting next spring and harvesting the winter wheat. Even the fruit trees stood a chance of bearing a small crop the following fall. I looked at our bounty and could not help but stand tall with pride. I hoped that Matilda could see it too, and knew that it was all worth the effort.

There was no time for rest—the harvest and planting of the winter wheat needed to happen. The weather was getting cooler by the day. Though the weather was mild, I knew there was no guarantee it would stay that way.

Harvest went by, and winter arrived. The first one was hard. The house was well-built and kept us warm. Taking care of the animals and keeping them warm was a never-ending chore. We purchased straw from Matilda's parents for bedding and rationed the animals' feed. The cattle, horses, and goats were allowed in the pasture at times. However, when the Midwest winter sent its worst, with strong winds and snow so fine that it felt like tiny needles against any bare skin, the animals were herded into the barn or any other structure where they could be penned. The chickens and ducks were not so lucky. They were always kept inside during the harsh weather, and more time spent indoors meant more manure. Winter was equally as busy, if not more so, than spring. All of us worked together to keep things running.

With all the preparation during Spring and harvest, we were able to live mostly on what we had raised ourselves. At times, we needed to buy flour and meat from town, along with the occasional thing we ran out of.

The winter passed slowly. We missed being outside and working in the warm sun; as a result, we felt pent-up and miserable. We all became easily aggravated. It became a test of our will not to argue. Matilda and I had books to keep us company and spent most of our evenings reading in front of the fireplace. Harold, however, was unable to read. He spent his time outside with the animals, finding things to keep himself busy between meals. The positive side of winter was that Matilda and I were able to start planning a family.

# Part 17: Our Second Spring

Part 17: Our Second Spring

By the time spring rolled around, we were happy to see the snow melt and the first signs of life sprout. It was March, and the chilly days started to warm. Discussions began for plowing more fields, planting our next crops, and harvesting winter wheat. Since we had a full season this year, we would plant even more crops than in our first year. As we were still showing a profit from the previous year, the debate over another hired man was also underway. We decided to build a small bunkhouse on the property to support the continued growth as well as provide some privacy for our employees. The future was looking bright!

I had noticed that Matilda had slowed down a bit over the last couple of months and seemed a bit unwell. She had not said anything, and I had not questioned her, although I was concerned. It was now April, and I thought the winter might have taken its toll on my beautiful wife. Early one morning, I awoke to hear her retching in the bathroom. Alarmed, I quickly ran to her side.

"What is wrong, my love?"

Matilda raised her head and attempted to clear her throat. She looked very pale, and her cheeks were ablaze with color. She took a moment longer to catch her breath before speaking, as if she did not want to worry me. "I have been suspicious for a while now and fear I may need to see a doctor to be sure. Cecil, I think we may be becoming parents." Though she still looked pale, she smiled weakly at me after the statement. Her joy was apparent even through her illness.

I could hardly believe my ears! Me, a father? Would I be a good father? I wanted a child, but how could I be a good parent with the upbringing I had endured? What would happen if this child disabled my beautiful Matilda, as I had disabled my mother when I was born? Worse yet, what if she did not survive the birth of the child? These and many more questions passed through my mind. I watched Matilda's face carefully as she waited for my reaction. She appeared scared. That thought, above all others, made me snap back to reality.

I quickly caught myself, for Matilda's sake, not allowing my thoughts to run away. I schooled my face to show none of my concerns, only the happiness and pride that any man should have when it was announced that he would be a new father.

"Cecil?" Her voice faltered, and her face drew with concern.

I quickly reached for her. She was still beside the toilet, trying her hardest not to retch again. I gently rubbed circles on her back.

"I could not be happier, my love! However, we must get you to the doctor immediately, and you MUST cut back on your work. We can afford to hire more help." I knew that part of the equation would be most challenging for her; however, in my eyes, it was not negotiable.

Concern eclipsed every obligation, and all plans for the day were set aside. I told Harold he was to oversee the chores, then helped Matilda into the Ford and headed for town to see the local doctor. I drove as quickly as the rutted road allowed, careful not to jostle her more than necessary. The trip felt far longer than it should have, stretched thin by worry, though I was driving faster than usual. Not a word passed between us. Matilda kept one hand pressed to her stomach, her fingers tense as if bracing for an answer she was not yet ready to hear, and stared out the window. I fixed my gaze on the road ahead, my thoughts churning in silence.

We arrived in town, and the Ford clattered to a halt. I insisted that Matilda wait while I informed the doctor of the situation. She began to balk, but quickly relented when she saw the pleading look on my face. I did not communicate it to her, but I believe she knew I had my own concerns I wanted to voice privately to the physician. The bell above the door rang as I entered the stuffy office. The rotund, bald-headed, older gentleman with brilliant blue eyes in a white coat ambled out of the back room and smiled at me.

"Cecil Amos, what can I do for you today, sir?"

I quickly explained the situation to the friendly man; he nodded as I spoke. I told him the story of my birth and that I was concerned for my wife. He assured me that he had delivered many babies in his time and boasted a great success rate. Though his kind words reassured me, I was still very concerned. He was able to fit us in right away. I felt slight relief at the thought of her at least being able to be examined right away. I rushed out the door to retrieve her and ushered her in the door slowly and carefully. I was instructed to wait in the small room where I had initially entered. I kissed my wife on the forehead and then sat.

Matilda smiled shyly. This was a look I had not seen since we had first met. "I will be all right, dear. Let the doctor do his job."

It was not long before I found myself pacing the front room, unable to sit still. I wanted to be with Matilda, every instinct urging me toward her. The thought of another man's hands on my wife—even a doctor's—set my nerves on edge. That unease tangled with deeper fears for her well-being and the fragile possibility of becoming a parent, until my thoughts raced in restless circles and threatened to overwhelm me.

The examination was quick but thorough. It was confirmed. Matilda was pregnant, and the doctor's best guess was that she was about four months along. All the long winter months played back in my memory, and I realized that December would have been about the right time for conception. At last, my fears were put to rest. The doctor assured us that he had no concerns about the pregnancy—Matilda was young, strong, and in good health. Relief flooded her face, bright and unmistakable, and when the doctor returned her to me, I felt as though the world had righted itself.

I could not rid myself of the feeling that something was going to go wrong. I hugged my bride, feigning the happiness I knew I should be feeling. I thanked the doctor and shook his hand. Matilda quickly locked arms with me as we exited his office. She appeared to be glowing.

We returned to the Ford, and began our trip back to the farm. I was again silent as we sat close together on the bench seat. As if she were able to read my mind, Matilda spoke, her voice trembling. "Cecil, won't you say something? Aren't you happy? The doctor has confirmed what we wanted and that I am healthy!"

I looked deeply into her eyes and could see how truly happy she was. Again, I was forced to change my demeanor for the sake of the woman I loved. I pasted a smile on my face. "Of course, I am happy, my love. What a wonderful turn of events!" With that, I tickled the her stomach where I now noticed a small bump had begun to grow, made her giggle. As we drove home, the doctor's reassurance did little to quiet the unease that clung to me. Joy sat easily on Matilda's face, but beneath my own smile something darker stirred, a nameless sense that this happiness rested on uncertain ground. I said nothing to her, keeping my voice light and my manner calm, while a silent warning coiled deep within me—unseen, unheard, and impossible to ignore.

Time after the announcement seemed to pass slowly. I hired an additional farmhand to help with chores and any other needs that may arise as the farm continued to grow and prosper. I would need to carefully split my time between working to build our future and ensuring that Matilda did not overdo anything. I was determined to keep her focused on her own well-being and that of our growing offspring. I knew this was a daunting task, as my beautiful bride was very independent and did not take well to having her activities limited. I hired a young woman to help with the cooking, housekeeping, and Matilda's trees and garden. Even with the additional assistance, Matilda insisted she be as active as possible. At times, this was more than what I agreed with, creating tension between the two of us.

"Cecil, why all this fuss? Women have babies every day without an issue. I will, too," Matilda protested.

I had just caught her in the cellar attempting to carry a heavy crate of canned vegetables to the pantry on the main level. For the first time since I had known her, it felt conflict brewing between us. My stubborn, strong-willed bride was insistent that she should be allowed to continue her normal activities despite being four months pregnant. I, being equally as stubborn, along with being a concerned first time father, was not about to allow her to harm herself or our unborn baby.

"Matilda, you know why. You know my family history. My only concern is for you," I pleaded, trying to convince her to listen.

"Argh! Cecil! I am not made of glass, and I am not your mother!" She dropped the crate of food. Most of the Ball jars full of last year's garden vegetables shattered as they hit the cellar's dirt floor. Her expression changed quickly from anger to shame as she looked at the mess she had made. She looked at me and then at the floor. Then she dropped to the floor and wept as she tried to clean the mess.

"Matilda... it's all right. There are more vegetables. Leave it now, before you cut yourself on the glass. I'll take care of it." I kept my voice calm and steady as I went to her, lifting her carefully to her feet as though she were already something fragile and precious. I guided her back to the main level and then up to our bedroom, settling her beneath the covers until she finally lay still.

I remained at her side, brushing my hand through her hair in slow, measured strokes, listening to her breathing until it evened and sleep claimed her at last. A quiet resolve took hold of me then—an understanding that I would have to watch her more closely now, shield her from even the smallest harm, whether she welcomed it or not. The thought sat heavy in my chest, carrying with it a warning I could not name.

Our second spring on the farm was unfolding with new life everywhere I looked. Calves arrived one by one in the fields, and with each birth, the weight of what I was preparing to protect grew heavier. I told myself it was only the natural worry of an expectant father, yet some deeper instinct whispered that the season ahead would demand more of me than I was ready to give.

A month later, I awoke from a fitful sleep. I had been dreaming. The images were a blur. All I could remember was an old woman. I seemed to remember her speaking to me in a warning voice, but I had forgotten what she had said. I knew I had slept, but I did not feel rested. I still needed to get up. It was the time of spring when most of the heifers were calving. Some required help as it was their first baby. All required checking multiple times a day. As I had a break from planting, my mornings were spent checking my cattle.

Matilda was still soundly asleep beside me. I watched the steady rise and fall of her chest as she slept peacefully. I carefully rose from our bed, attempting not to disturb her. I tiptoed to our bathroom and quickly used the commode. Then, I went to the sink, washed my hands, and splashed cold water on my face multiple times until I finally felt more awake. Still groggy, I brushed my hair and teeth and dressed in my work clothes, ready to start my day.

Coffee was already brewing in the kitchen, and our house helper had started making a batch of eggs. Bacon sizzled in the pan next to it. I plopped down heavily onto one of the kitchen chairs with a sigh, rubbing my weary eyes. After having a cup of coffee, I started to feel the drowsiness from a restless night slowly fading away. After breakfast, the effects of the restless sleep were all but gone.

Something nagged at me. Matilda was still not up. *It's no reason to be concerned. It's good for her to be getting her rest.* I thought to myself, trying to reassure myself that there was no reason to be alarmed. I decided to go about my chores and check on her once the animals had ben cared for if she was still not up. I thanked my house help for breakfast as she started cleaning up, and headed for the door. I grabbed my hat from the hook on the wall and placed it firmly on my head, setting off briskly toward the shed containing the heifers.

The heifers and the bull were kept separately when the bull's services were not needed.

As I walked towards the barn, I heard the distressed bellow. It was loud enough for me to detect long before I got close to the barn. I picked up my pace, breaking into a run, knowing that the sound meant that one of the heifers was having trouble. I quickly reached the shed. I stopped at the door listening, and looking around at each animal to see where the sound was coming from. In the very corner of the shed was one of the black heifers lying on her side, breathing heavily. She craned her neck, raising her head and letting out another cry as if begging for help. Her eyes rolled back in her head as it fell to the ground. I knew from her movements that it was too late to get help; I was going to have to pull this calf or lose both the mother and the baby.

Without further hesitation, I knelt at her side, examining her. I felt her hardened abdomen with gentle hands. It felt as if the calf was turned the wrong way. As I worked to turn the calf, the heifer continued to push and bellow in agony. I was finally able to turn the calf, allowing the heifer to evacuate it from her body with one final push. I removed the remainder of the amniotic sac from the newborn calf's nostrils, willing it to breathe with all my might. It was to no avail. The labor had taken too long, and I was there too late. I looked down at the stillborn baby; disappointment and sadness washed over me. I was exhausted from my efforts, and defeated due to not being able to save the calf. I breathed a heavy sigh, knowing my task was not yet complete.

My attention turned back to the mother, knowing there was nothing else I could do for the little one. I got the mother up and quickly checked her for any signs of further distress. Satisfied that she was in no physical danger, I turned her out into the pasture. I could see that she was distraught, but there was nothing I could do to help her. The heifer tried multiple times to get back into the barn through the gate to her baby. The site was heart-wrenching. Now, she sadly bellowed nonstop. I picked the calf up, hefting it over my shoulder. On my way out of the shed, I grabbed a shovel in my free hand. I walked towards a corner of the pasture where no animals were kept. I laid the now cold calf down and began to dig. As I did, the same feeling I had earlier returned. I shivered as the feeling that the dream had left returned. I thought of Matilda and our unborn child, hoping that the dream, the death of the calf, and my unborn child were unrelated.

I carefully laid the baby calf in the grave and shoveled the dirt back on him. I had checked the other heifers while in the barn, so for the moment, nothing else needed my immediate attention. I felt dirty. As I looked down at my arms, I realized that they were covered with blood, dirt, and sweat. I needed a shower. I dragged my feet back to the house, defeated at my failure weighing down each slow step.

As I turned to head to the house, the door opened, and a smiling Matilda waltzed out. She stopped in her tracks when she saw me. "Cecil, what happened?"

I realized my appearance must have been very startling, aand immediately tried to quiet her concern. "I'm all right, Matilda."

Then the heifer bellowed again. Matilda seemed to realize what had happened. She looked from me, still holding the shovel and covered in blood, to the newly dug grave in the pasture.

"Oh, you poor thing," she cried in anguish, heading for the fence where the agitated heifer stood.

"Matilda, don't!" I yelled after her.

What happened next seemed to happen in slow motion. Before I could stop her, Matilda closed the gap between herself and the pasture. Although she had grown up on a farm and knew better, her motherly instincts took over. She lifted the bottom wire of the fence, slid herself under it, and was walking towards the heifer. The heifer bellowed again, this time, a warning. The heifer's head went down, her eyes wild with anger, and she charged Matilda. I dropped my shovel and ran towards her. I couldn't get there quickly enough. I heard the sickening thud as the heifer's large black head connected directly with Matilda's pregnant belly. I screamed as I ran towards the animal and my wife. Matilda flew like a rag doll through the air and landed near the fence. She was stunned; however, she had enough peace of mind to roll under the fence, away from the heifer.

I rushed to her side. There were no visible injuries on her body, but she had curled up into the fetal position and held her stomach in pain. She closed her eyes as I reached her.

"Cecil...help me...." came the painful words. Then she blacked out. I was terrified!

I quickly scooped her up in my arms and rushed her to the Ford, gently laying her motionless body in the back seat. I drove to town as quickly as the Ford would allow. I hit the brakes hard as I pulled up to the doctor's office. He must have heard the commotion as he met me outside.

"Cecil, what is it?" the old doctor asked, seeing the alarm on my face.

"It's Matilda! She was attacked by one of the heifers! She rolled under the fence to escape and then blacked out! I got her here as quickly as I could!" He helped me get the love of myself inside. I could see that he was as concerned as I was. This time, he did not try to quell my fears; he simply acted.

Once the doctor and I had gotten Matilda inside and onto the examining room table, I was forced to leave. The doctor did not want me to distract him as he examined her. It seemed like hours as I paced the floor outside the closed door, waiting for word.

The door opened with a creak. Slowly, the doctor emerged, looking exhausted with a serious look on his face. I paused, knowing that the news could not be good. The doctor approached me and laid a gentle hand on my shoulder. He looked down as he spoke. "I am sorry. Matilda is fine, but she has lost the baby. I will need to keep her overnight to ensure there are no complications."

I felt as if my world had stopped spinning. I had just come to terms with being a new father, and Matilda was safely through the first portion of her pregnancy. Now, it was over. I didn't know what to say or how to react. Slowly, I spoke. "May I see her?"

"She is resting now. The process of losing the baby is equally taxing on a woman as birthing a live child. I have given her a sedative, which will allow her to rest. It will make her very groggy. You may sit with her, but I would advise you not to wake her."

I could not find the words to say. What felt like a large lump had lodged in my throat. I refused to allow the doctor to see me break down despite all the emotions. With that, I squared my shoulders, nodded to the doctor, and ushered myself to the room where my wife lay asleep.

I sat with Matilda in the hard wicker chair throughout the night, never touching her or making a sound. She had not moved since my entry to the room. I assumed the medication, along with her exhaustion, caused her to sleep continually. I slept fitfully in small durations. I wanted to ensure I was there and fully alert when she woke up.

The next day was long. She awoke late in the afternoon, groaning in pain. She blinked, licked her chapped lips, and slowly pushed herself upright in the bed. Then she looked around at her surroundings. As she looked in my direction, her wide eyes focused on me.

"Cecil, what happened?" she asked, clearly confused and in pain.

I fought back my own pain, trying decide how to tell her as I made my way to her. I placed my hand gently on her shoulder, willing her to lie back down. I could feel the physical and mental anguish radiating from her. Her hair was tangled and frizzy, loose around her shoulders, and her eyes were puffy. To me, she was still the most beautiful woman I had ever laid eyes on.

"What is the last thing you remember?" I asked gently.

I realized I must have looked like a mess. The remnants of the night before were still on my clothing, and I must also smell horrible. I backed away for a moment, allowing her to try to process.

Matilda squinted, pinching the bridge of her nose, trying to piece together what had happened in her mind. "I remember waking up and having breakfast. Our housemaid said you had gone outside to tend the heifers. I was going to come out to check on you..." Then her voice trailed off, and her gaze became distant as if she had remembered. "I lost the baby, didn't I?"

# Part 18: Moving On

Part 18: Moving On

After we had got home, and I got Matilda settled in our bed, I sent Harold to her parents' home. They needed to know that they had lost their grandchild, and we needed their support. They did not hesitate to drop everything and com to the aid of myself and their beloved daughter. I was relieved that she would have her parents to help her cope. With the hired help, and aid of my in-laws, I could deal with the loss myself, and be with my wife to help her recover. I had sent a letter back home to my uncles to let them know what had happened and to asked them to inform the rest of the family.

Matilda was very depressed, blaming herself for the loss of the baby. Most days, she did not move out of our bed. I tried my best to be an empathetic husband. I brought her pain medication and food. I helped her out of bed to keep her clean and use the commode. I did my best to reassure her that the loss of our child was not her fault.

I, too, was struggling. I was careful not to let this show in front of my wife. I began having nightly dreams in which an old woman spoke to me in a different tongue. Each morning, I tried to recall and write down the dream. Every time I reviewed my notes, the description was the same. The woman looked familiar, but her message remained unclear to me. Her visits became ever more disturbing.

This went on for an entire month. I was becoming irritable. Even as a patient and understanding man, I had my limits. We lost the baby. It was time we moved on together. There had to be a way to deal with this. That morning, I awoke, leaving Matilda alone. I went through my morning routine and left without saying a word.

I had decided to take things into my own hands. I arrived at the doctor's office. To my relief, there was no one else present. I sat down heavily in front of his desk, realizing I must have looked as exhausted as I felt. I ran my hand through my hair and tried to gather my thoughts before I started. He looked at me, concerned, as I discussed our problem with him. He agreed that a change was needed. He was to pay a visit to our home the following day. We would not allow her to just fade away into her own world. I needed her.

Unfortunately, there was no medical treatment. The doctor would visit our home, do an examination, and give Matilda the information when nothing physical was found. All we could do was hope that the reassurance that her physical health was fine, as well as the possibility of conceiving again, would be enough to bring her back to reality.

I realized what I was doing seemed callous. I had no idea what else to do. Somehow, we had to move past this. I knew it would not happen all at once, but hoped that with the doctor's help, life could begin to return to normal. I hoped that since she had healed physically, Matilda could begin to mend mentally. I returned home with new hope. I had determined that everyone, except our hired help, would return to their everyday lives, forcing Matilda to do things for herself again.

With the doctor's reassurance, Matilda did begin to improve. She was a changed woman, becoming much quieter. She insisted that our housekeeper be let go so she could return to caring for our home. She also began spending great amounts of time working in the orchard and her garden. She pulled away from me almost entirely, crushing my hopes that we could be happy again. She continued making our meals, and we still slept in the same bed. However, the closeness that was once there had all but disappeared. There were no more sweet kisses, no more long conversations, and no more gentle touches. I took it in stride as best I could, never completely losing hope. As she threw herself into the orchard, I threw myself into the farm.

The farm continued to prosper despite our faltering relationship. I was reminded of my parents. From the outside looking in, all was well. Most nights after coming in from work, I sat alone in the kitchen, my head in my palms, wondering where I had gone wrong.

I tried speaking to Matilda. She was always kind but seemed very detached. Her responses were clipped and professional, almost as if she were speaking to someone she barely knew, not someone she loved. My patience was wearing thin. I didn't know what else to do for her. I was distraught. I loved her, but I felt shut out. Our once-warm home felt more like an iceberg.

Her beautiful face seemed to age years within just a few months. Fine lines appeared around her mouth and eyes, and deeper lines appeared on her forehead. I wondered if she saw the same on my face. The loss of our child had hurt us both deeply.

I suggested we wait some time to heal and then try again. Her face had gone red at the suggestion. She did not respond; she only picked up a broom and began sweeping the wooden floor. She did not think I noticed, but I saw a tear trickle down her face and heard a slight sniffle. I walked over to her, feeling the anguish, and wrapped my arms around her, trying to reassure her.

"Cecil, don't," was the response I received.

I quickly withdrew, hurt by the rejection. I stomped towards the door, slamming my hat on my head, and went outside, with no destination other than away from the tension inside my home in mind. I knew that I would be sleeping on the loveseat that evening.

There was a bitter irony in it all. I found myself beginning to understand my father in ways I never wished to. The pull toward cruelty—toward resentment and retaliation—rose unbidden, and I was unsettled by how readily it answered me. When I went into town alone, that awareness followed close behind. It may have been my imagination, yet the glances lingered longer than before, smiles came too easily, and I felt, unmistakably, that some of the women were seeing me not as a married man, but as an invitation—one I refused to acknowledge, even as its presence troubled me deeply.

I found myself recounting my childhood and how much I had hated watching my father's bitterness toward my mother. I wondered if there may have been two sides to the story. Had she shut my father out after I was born? Was I too young to remember? I now knew the grief of losing a child. Was my mother's grief at losing her mobility enough to cause her to shut my father out and make him feel the way I was feeling now?

The thought was disturbing. I knew how he had reacted. I decided then and there that I would be better, no matter how much it hurt me. I continued throwing myself into my work, giving Matilda space to heal. I would also put forth the same effort I had when we were courting. I would take my cues from her and make sure to keep my own emotions in check.

We had another beautiful spring with plentiful rain and no severe weather. The pastures were flush with grass, allowing the animals to be fat, happy, and well-watered. The crops grew well.

Spring went by, and the planting was done. Harold moved into the bunkhouse with the newly hired man, sensing that we needed our space. The winter wheat was harvested, and we put up some hay. Even with the loss of the calf, we had a fine crop of new babies. Some would be kept, and some would be sold. There were a few we could butcher for our own use this year.

I started going to town once a week and brought home something from the local eatery for our evening meal. I made sure that on this day of the week, the chores were done early, and I was inside. At first, Matilda objected. I allowed it. I sat and ate alone on these occasions, allowing her to make whatever food she wanted for herself. On other days, I would bring fresh wildflowers and leave them on the counter. For a while, they just sat there. I bought a record player for our home and some of her favorite songs. I would leave it playing when I left the house to work on the farm. I also surprised her by working late into the evening, placing landscaping around each tree in her orchard to keep the weeds down and retain moisture.

I watched her reactions, hoping my actions would bring us closer. I had not forgotten what made her happy. It was my intention to bring enough of those things to her, that she would remember as well. Initially, I started to see occasional smiles, though they were hidden from me. Then the flowers began moving around the house and being cared for. The music played even when I did not start it. I caught a glimpse of her dancing a jig as she cleaned the kitchen one day. Finally, it happened. She joined me at the table when I brought home our weekly meal. We sat quietly and ate our first meal together in months. There was no conversation, no argument, nor the tense feeling that had been hanging over us.

That evening, to my surprise and great pleasure, she curled up against me in our bed. I cautiously responded, placing an arm around her and pulling her closer. I smiled, closing my eyes contentedly, and falling into peaceful sleep with her beside me. It seemed things were finally looking up. Maybe we had made it. Maybe things could finally move in the right direction.

# Part 19: Things Begin to Turn

Part 19: Things Begin to Turn

As Matilda and I recovered, the farm flourished. We hired another man full-time, freeing up more time for us. Matilda allowed me to hire her house help back, giving her more time to relax. The age lines that had begun to show on her face faded. The one thing we had not been able to achieve together was conceiving another child. As time passed, it seemed we were doomed to be barren.

Things began to change in the summer of 1929, specifically the weather. The rains were few and far between. It became so hot that the air was thick and hard to breathe. We got no break, yet we continued with the chores as usual. Each day was miserable, to say the least. Our clothes stuck to our bodies, and the thick dust stuck to them, turning every garment we owned a sludgy gray.

The crops struggled. Dust seemed to be everywhere. Some days, it was so thick that a person could barely see the nose on his own face. Then came the clouds of grasshoppers descending upon everything. They ruined the beans and corn and decimated the already dry pastureland. Matilda's garden and our winter food supply were also affected, leaving us concerned for our well-being. Even the fruit trees and their flowers were not safe. It seemed the little bastards would eat anything!

The animals lost weight due to the lack of nutrition, and we quickly burned through the feed we had left from the prior winter. Soon, we were forced to order feed from surrounding states and had it shipped in at a premium expense by train. We bought what we could from town to keep weight on the cattle and keep the teams of horses fit to work the land. The stock pond in the pasture began to dry up, and the wells throughout our property were at the lowest levels I had ever seen. We were careful to ensure the animals received only the water they needed to survive. We also rationed our water indoors. Baths were allowed once a week. Aside from that, a jug and a cloth were kept next to the sink for wiping off. We brushed our teeth once a day, using a splash of water from the same jug. Despite Matilda's best efforts, along with the hired help, the house always seemed to be clouded with dust. It aggravated our lungs, causing coughing, a runny nose, and sneezing, which became a constant part of our lives. I dug out an outhouse and put up walls around it to be used as much as possible instead of the indoor plumbing we had become accustomed to. I was prepared to do whatever was necessary to protect our livelihood. Inconveniences meant nothing when compared to the risk of losing it all. The land seemed to follow the pattern of our attempt to bear a child. It, too, seemed doomed to become barren.

For the first time, that year, we lost money on our farm. Crop prices were down, and we had to sell animals. I feared that if the following year was not any better, we would have to start selling portions of the farm.

The weight of it pressed down on me until it was hard to breathe. Night after night, after a sparse supper, I remained at the kitchen table with pencil and paper, my fingers tangled in my hair as I stared at the figures that refused to obey reason. What more could I possibly do to keep from losing everything we had sacrificed to build? I erased and recalculated until the paper grew thin, yet the sums still would not balance.

Had I rushed headlong into this life? Poured too much into the land itself? Should I have kept the farm smaller, hoarded what remained of my father's money and my own hard-won profits? The questions came without mercy, circling in the dark long after the lamp had burned low. None of it made sense—none of it followed the rules I had learned on the prosperous family farm back east. And yet, despite doing everything as I had been taught, a cold certainty settled in my gut: something unseen was working against me, and no amount of careful planning would be enough to stop it.

We sold all but the basic stock needed that year before winter, keeping only the breeding stock for our cattle, two milk cows, and one hog, which would be kept for butchering when needed. We sold all the goats and the Quarter Horses, keeping only the team of Draft Horses. We kept a handful of chickens and a few ducks to ensure we still had a source of meat and eggs. I did not plant anything to be harvested the following spring. With these changes, we no longer needed additional help. We cut back the farm help to just two hired men: Harold and a younger man. We reduced the house help to working twice a week. The two farmhands moved into the main residence, and the housemaid maintained her residence in town. The bunkhouse was left empty.

After making these changes, I was once again able to balance our farm budget, though it would make for a very long winter. Just as I was beginning to relax a bit, it became worse. I had gone to town to take care of my monthly banking. Upon arriving, I could see that something was amiss. It seemed that the entire town was in an uproar. People were yelling, and arguing amongst themselves. As I passed what used to be my store, someone crashed through a window. I stopped the car abruptly and exited quickly towards the man, now lying crumpled on the ground. I checked on the man, who groaned as I turned him on his back to examine him. He appeared to be mostly intact, aside from some minor cuts that I assumed must have come from going through the plate-glass window. I let him lie and quickly entered the store, allowing the door to slam behind me.

The young man who now ran my father's store stood near the window and immediately recognized me. "Mr. Amos, did you hear?" he panted. It was clear he had tussled with the man outside, causing the man to fall through the window.

"Hear what, son?" I asked, now very concerned.

"The stock markets have crashed. Our money is no longer good! I had folks in here trying to loot the store since word got out! The whole town is a mess! The bank is the worst, and I don't blame em!" His words tumbled quickly from his mouth. He wiped the sweat from his brow and looked at me as if I were about to harm him.

I stood frozen. I had no idea what to do. The implications were clear. Bad had now gone to worse. There was no purpose in my attempting to do my business. At no fault of my own, we were broke despite all of my efforts to cut back and remain afloat! I was devastated! We would have to live off of what we had for the foreseeable future. I knew I would have to tell Matilda, which would burden her further.

At risk of losing my composure, I chose to leave the store and return home to face what needed to be done. Without a word, I turned on my heel, stomped back to my car, and sped back to our farm. I was glad we had been able to sell as much as we could, stocked our cellar with canned goods, and saved as much feed as possible. It would have to be enough to get us through winter now. If the stock market indeed crashed, which, by all indications, it had, the small amount of money we had in the bank was gone. All we had left was the cash stashed in a coffee can at home. Even that may do us no good. We would need to rely heavily on each other and our hired help to stand any chance of making it through the winter. We would deal with spring and planting as they came.

I pulled into the yard near the house, tires kicking up dust and making a scraping sound as I skidded to a halt. "Matilda!" I yelled.

I heard her running through the house, and then she appeared on the porch quickly. Seeing my face, hers mirrored my alarm. "Cecil! What has happened?"

"We are in trouble! The stock market crashed, and the town is in ruin! Our money is no longer good! What we have now is what we will need to make do with for the foreseeable future."

With that, the remaining staff were gathered and assured they had a home with us as long as we could afford them. We set to work on taking inventory of what we had. We rounded up the remaining stock and penned them on the ten acres nearest the barn so that all of them had access to shelter. The remaining outbuildings would not be used.

Thankfully, Matilda's garden was not a complete loss. We managed to salvage most of the root vegetables, though they were far smaller than they should have been. There were carrots, onions, potatoes, and beets—enough for her to can and add to what remained of the previous year's stores. We also saved a modest portion of fruit from the trees, harvesting it early and allowing it to finish ripening in the cellar before canning it as well. With a careful rationing of sugar, the preserves would quiet the craving for sweets and offer what nourishment they could.

We were relieved—almost giddy—to realize there was enough food to carry us through the winter, provided it was not too severe and we rationed carefully. The chickens continued to lay despite the lack of proper nesting, offering eggs for protein and, if necessary, meat from the roosters. For now, the cows still gave milk, which meant butter as well. By any measure, we were better off than many.

What sustained us most, however, was faith. It allowed us to look squarely at our circumstances and understand that, though times were hard, we were among the fortunate. We could endure.

Some trees in the grove surrounding our farm had died from a lack of water. The wood was not yet dried; however, we began cutting and stacking what we could. Thankfully, I had the foresight to have our home built with a fireplace and a wood-burning stove for cooking. At the time, these things seemed more of a convenience, but now, with the lack of commodities, I was grateful I had done so.

We gathered containers of any type, filling them with fresh, well water to be rationed. We ensured our home was secure, as it was well known in the area that we had been wealthy prior to this crisis. Each of us owned a firearm and was instructed to keep it nearby. The reality was that those we had called neighbors and friends may now become the enemy. Disaster had struck, and we knew we would be tested.

# Part 20: Winter 1929 and The Year 1930

Part 20: Winter 1929 and The Year 1930

A rough summer turned into a rougher winter. The winter of 1929-1930 was the worst I had experienced. With much of the prairie ravaged by drought, the snow seemed to have nowhere to stick. More snow fell each day, and the wind blew harder. Despite our home being well-built, it still felt as if the wind was blowing through the walls at times. We wore multiple layers to keep warm and kept the stove burning as much as possible, without depleting our supply to the point of panic.

When going outdoors to do the chores, coveralls, an additional coat, and a pair of wool socks were added to the wardrobe. A rope was run from the house to the barn so that we could find the barn on the worst of the wintery blizzard days. With snow so fine and thick, it was all I could do to open my eyes when making my way back and forth between the buildings, but the animals needed care. We needed the animals. There was no choice. Some days, it was so cold that ice formed on my eyelashes.

Eventually, the snow began to cling to the ground. In some ways, it was a blessing—keeping the animals watered in the bitter cold had become nearly impossible. I boiled water on the stove and carried it down to the barn in endless trips, the buckets sometimes crusting with ice before I even reached the door. Once the snow stayed, the animals could at least eat it for moisture.

But this snow was unlike any I had known. It never truly hardened. Instead, it stayed loose and grainy beneathfoot, shifting and sinking like pale quicksand, treacherous in its stillness.

We were unable to make it to town for several months. The housemaid stopped coming because she could no longer make the trip, leaving full responsibility on Matilda, the hired men, and me. Our little family was now down to the four of us, making rationing easier but doubling the work around the farm.

Each day stretched longer than the one before it. Talk of bringing a child into the world gave way to quiet calculations about how we might survive the winter. In the midst of it all, Matilda grew stronger, steadier, while I began to fray. The loss of our child, the hard turn in the weather, and the mounting financial strain pressed down on me until endurance gave way to exhaustion. I had fought through each blow as it came, but every man has his limit. I had reached mine.

It was I who began to unravel. Each morning, when I faced my reflection, the changes were unmistakable. Though I was not yet middle-aged, my hair thinned more with every passing day, gray threading through what had once been a thick black mane.

I grew quiet and withdrawn, trapped within my own thoughts. It felt as though history was repeating itself from the days after we lost our child—only now the roles were reversed. This time, it was Matilda urging me onward, steady where I was faltering. I had nothing left to give her.

Once more, that shadow of understanding crept into my mind. Before, I had measured myself against my father and recoiled at the resemblance. Now I found myself weighing my fragile state against Matilda's in her own worst hour—and finding myself wanting in ways that unsettled me. She had never yielded. Each day she cooked and cleaned, her smile unwavering. Each day she spoke words meant to lift me. Each day, I took what strength I could from her. Yet with every kindness she offered, something in me tightened rather than eased, a quiet pressure building beneath the surface—one that made me fear not what I might lose, but what I was becoming.

How could this be happening to us? How could our well-thought-out plan become such a nightmare? What curse had been placed upon us to lose a child and now to face the possibility of losing everything we had worked for? I knew, realistically, that we were lucky to be in the position we were in. We weren't left hungry, nor were we near the point of running out of supplies. Though thin, our animals were still alive. We had everything we needed, yet I could not fight the anger.

Regret began to seep into my thoughts, slow and unwelcome. I found myself looking back to the life I had left in the East. There, I had security, money, and a family to fall back on—even if my father's cruelty had cast a long shadow. I had a future laid out before me, a clear understanding of what was expected and how to succeed.

In quieter moments, I dared to ask myself questions I did not want answered. If I had never met Matilda, would I have stayed here at all? The land I had once believed to be the most beautiful I had ever seen now felt increasingly barren, even forsaken. And from that bitterness, resentment began to take shape. Was she the reason I stood here struggling—clinging to survival—when comfort and prosperity might have been mine without effort, had I simply followed the path my father had chosen for me?

The thought sickened me even as it lingered, unwelcome yet impossible to dismiss.

A bitter taste rose from my gut to my throat. I closed my eyes and took a deep breath, forcing my thoughts to settle in a better place. The woman was doing everything she could and working equally as hard as the hired men and me. She was suffering, too. I took another deep breath, forced myself to open my eyes, and focused on her. There she stood, humming as she wiped down the countertop in the kitchen with a threadbare, filthy rag. I inhaled deeply. The scent of the stew cooking on the wood stove filled my nostrils. I forced myself back to reality. I had a good woman. I could be like poor Harold, with no family and no woman, only us to call his family. I mustn't allow the negativity of this world to overtake me.

Fast forward several months. We had made it through the winter, yet things did not seem to improve. The weather went from snow and blizzards back to heat and drought in the blink of an eye. The spring of 1930 had not brought prosperity back. Instead, the snow that had stung our eyes and lungs was replaced again with dust. We could not afford to skip planting another year, nor could our supplies last without replenishment. The odds of a bountiful harvest as we had seen in the past were low, but what had to be done, had to be done. We went about planting as best we could; however, it was slow, and we had only three men and one team of horses. With the wind and the blowing dust, more of the costly seed was blowing away than staying in the neatly plowed rows.

Despite the severity of our circumstances, necessity left no room for hesitation. We pressed on, managing to till and plant barely half the acreage we had intended after heavy losses of seed. All we could do was hope that what remained in the ground would be enough to turn a profit—assuming there would still be buyers left after such a brutal winter.

Matilda dug her garden by hand, as there was no time to spare to help her. Wiser from the year before, she planted only below-ground crops. We set aside a small sum for spray for the fruit trees, clinging to the hope that enough might survive to sell. She did everything that needed doing without complaint, yet she grew noticeably quieter with each passing day. I could feel her unhappiness building beneath the surface and feared what might come if her despair returned. At the same time, I feared my own bitterness would no longer stay hidden. Between us, something volatile was forming—a pressure not unlike the dust storms that swept the land each day, unseen at first, then impossible to escape.

The chickens were allowed to sit on their eggs in hopes of having more chickens. We were down to one rooster after we had been forced to butcher the others. We were still hanging on to the one sow we had left and had allowed her to be bred back. The dairy cattle had their little ones, ensuring we would have fresh milk. The new life, though bringing more mouths to feed, brought with it the hope of selling a few more animals in the fall when the dust storms allowed.

Though we all got along well, we still needed social interaction. The town was suffering as badly as the country was. Buildings were beginning to fall into disrepair due to the harsh weather. The bank was open; however, there did not seem to be a point with the state of the economy. Those who had money kept cash. It seemed most had resorted to trading. The General Store, which I had worked so hard to bring back to life, was beginning to look as it had before I took over. The shelves were bare, and the young man who had taken over struggled to open the door each day. People were pulling up stakes and moving on.

As for our little family unit, we were determined to stay. We had more assets we could sell if need be. I was not about to give up. The fall harvest would tell a lot about what the future would hold. The weather had to change for the better at some point, after all. The stock market had to come back up. Things would normalize. They had to. When they did, I would still be hanging on.

# Part 21: 1931

Part 21: 1931

I had been dreadfully wrong. The Great Depression, as it was now being called, had continued. We butchered most of the animals. We no longer had any horses to work the land. We had sold off what we could, piece by piece. Now, nothing was left other than the house, the barn, and the ten acres surrounding it. Still, I was determined not to give up.

Matilda had aged. So had I. Yet, she still did her best to stay cheerful. Each night, she used what she had to make some sort of bare-bones meal for us. We had let our other hired man go, and now only Harold remained with us. The East and West Coasts had not been hit as hard by the weather and hardships as the Midwest. Word had gotten out that land was being sold for pennies on the dollar just so that folks could leave. City folks were buying up everything we had worked so hard to build.

The anger continued to build, heavy and unrelenting. I could not understand what I had done to deserve it, only that the punishment—whatever its origin—grew harsher with each passing day, as though some judgment had already been passed long before I was aware of it. My thoughts returned, again and again, to my father. Perhaps his circumstances had not merely shaped him, but carried him along a path he could never step off. Perhaps there was only so much hurt a man could endure before something within him fractured. I had spent years believing that I could choose differently, that will alone could sever me from what came before. Now that belief was eroding. The harder I resisted, the more it felt as though I were fulfilling something already set in motion, moving toward an end I could sense but no longer avoid.

Matilda's positive attitude continued becoming more of an annoyance to me. I had no idea how she could be so positive while watching our world collapse. I felt that happiness was simply not meant for us.

After another bare-bones supper of boiled vegetables with a few meat scraps, I could no longer take it. Matilda placed her hand on my shoulder as she picked up my bowl from the table. She began to hum as she walked towards the sink, full of dishes that could not be washed because there was no water.

"Woman!" I roared, "How can you continue to be so happy?"

111

She stopped in her tracks, frozen by the sudden onslaught of my rage. "Cecil?"

"No, that is enough! I cannot stand the sound of your voice any longer!" I rose from my chair quickly, causing it to fall back onto the floor with a crash. I closed the distance between us in just a few long strides, raised my hand, and slapped her sharply across the face.

Matilda gasped, and tears began rolling down her face silently. It was as if she were in shock. She did not react, aside from becoming completely silent and raising her hand to her now bruised face. I stood and watched as she continued on about the task she had started without a word.

As I watched her, what I had done struck me. I had done something I had often watched my father do to my beloved mother. Something I had sworn I would never do myself. I had allowed my frustration to get the better of me and struck my beloved wife. Waves of shame washed over me. I could no longer bear to be in the same house as her. She had done nothing to deserve this. She could not control the weather nor our lack of money. I turned and headed towards the door, allowing it to slam behind me. I knew I needed to go.

That night was the beginning of the end. I knew what I was doing was wrong, but I could no longer control myself. It was as if some external force had taken ahold of me and my mind said one thing, while my body did something different. Something more violent. Each day, I sat in the house with nothing to do but try to find a way out. Each night was sleepless. Due to a lack of money, I could no longer drive to town. Due to the awful dust, I could not even take a walk to ease my mind. It seemed our lives had become our own version of hell. A hell which I could not escape. I could not help but blame Matilda.

Trapped inside with her, the walls closing in day after day, my anger swelled until it eclipsed reason entirely. The rational part of my mind withered, just as the crops outside had withered, leaving only something raw and desperate behind. I told myself I needed release—some way to bleed off the pressure before it crushed me. At first, I lashed out in moments I barely recognized as my own. When she resisted, when she dared to remind me that she still possessed a will of her own, something inside me hardened. I could not allow that.

What followed felt unreal, as though I were watching my own hands move from a great distance. The cellar became a place I could not think about without nausea. Even as I acted, a voice inside me screamed in protest. *This is Matilda. This is the woman you love.*

When the rage passed, it left only shame in its wake—thick, suffocating, inescapable. I told myself I would stop. I told myself I would set things right, that this was not who I was meant to be. Yet the truth pressed in from all sides: I was becoming my father. The very thing I had fled across the country to escape was now wearing my own face. I wondered then—too late—whether I had ever truly been running *away*, or merely running *toward* the same end by another road.

Eventually, Matilda threatened to leave. I had continued the beatings, trying desperately to ease my pain. Now, I was chaining her to her beloved pear tree, as it was the largest and most sturdy of the trees left on our property. When this began, I only let her go with the threat that I would kill her if she tried to escape or tell anyone.

As if history were repeating itself, she, like my mother, hid the bruises with clothing or her hair as best she could. I could see the terror on her face when I came near. It tore me to pieces, but still, now that I had started, I could not stop. Hitting her was the only release I had. I knew we were in debt. I knew we would lose the farm. It was only a matter of time now.

Neither Matilda nor I ever went to town. One by one, our friends disappeared—some forced away by circumstance, others driven off by my own unkindness. Left alone with my thoughts, I felt the boundaries of myself begin to blur. I asked the question I had long avoided: was I still Cecil, or had I become Cedric?

Matilda's parents had both passed away one right after the other a year or so ago. They, too, had been bankrupted by this new way of life. Bankrupt and heartbroken, like so many of us. Pride kept me from contacting my parents for help. I had cut ties. I was not about to let them know that I had failed. My Uncles and Aunt still wrote, but I did not communicate back. Now, all we had was each other. We were all trapped in the same circle of HELL.

I tried to handle what business was left with Harold's help. He had moved into town, unable to bear witness to what I was doing, yet for some unknown reason, he remained loyal. He brought the meager supplies we needed and could afford from town. To the outside world, nothing was any different for us than any other struggling farmer.

As I continued to torture myself, running the numbers and trying to figure out what else I could sell aside from the remainder of the farm itself, the abuse got worse. I started locking Matilda in the cellar when I did not have her chained to that pear tree she loved so much. I couldn't stand to hear her or even look at her.

Her once large, strong frame was shrinking. She was no longer making the meals. I was making what I knew how to make out of the little supplies we had left and what we could barely afford to buy. Matilda was only allowed to eat my scraps. She was slowly starving and wasting away. I was, too. Physically and mentally, each day became worse. How was I to escape this loop of hurt and suffering?

The one thing I knew for certain was that if Matilda and I could not live out our dreams here together, no one else should be allowed to either. I'd be damned if I let the bank have this property while I was still alive. A notice from the bank arrived, telling me it had come to precisely that. Due to poor crops and the poor economy, the money had dried up. I had been forced to take out a loan to make ends meet. The notices had been coming, saying the loan was due. Now, I have received the final notice, giving us thirty days to be off our property.

I screamed, a guttural roar similar to that of a wounded animal that knew it was dying. I violently tore the notice to shreds, knowing there was nothing I could do. As I stood and stared at the shredded paper, realization came that there was only one thing left to do.

I went to the room that Matilda and I used to share so happily. I reached under my pillow, grasping the cold, solid object. This revolver had traveled with me from the East Coast. It had been given to me by my father, the man I detested yet had become so much like. It had served me well over the years, and now I needed it to serve me one last time. There was no other solution. No way out without giving what was mine to someone else. It all needed to end.

It seemed as if nothing around me existed any longer. I felt as if I were in a daze as I descended the stairs and exited the house, slowly approaching the tree where Matilda had been chained. Then it happened.

I screamed at her as I approached. I held nothing back. "You did this! You! This is all your fault! You convinced me to stay out here. I had it all. I would have inherited my father's business by now. Instead, I am out here in the dirty,

God-forsaken prairie, working my hands to the bone like I never have before in all my life, and still failing! All because you wanted a farm!" I was seeing red. Forgotten were my dreams and the real reason I forged my life in the Midwest. I had completely lost control.

Matilda looked at me helplessly, too tired to fight back. She was chained to the tree. I could hear her pleading. Her hands above her head were raw and bleeding. Her legs buckled, no longer able to support her weight. Tears streamed down her dirty, bruised face.

Then it happened. I stopped yelling. I looked at her with a blank look in my eyes. A maniacal laugh escaped my lips. I reached behind my back, producing the small revolver. It was as if I watched the scene unfold through someone else's eyes, not committing the act myself.

"Please, Cecil!" I heard her cry. "Please don't hurt me more. We can sell the rest and move back east. I'm sure your parents would still have a job for you. I can cook and clean for whoever needs the help."

Though I heard her, I could not stop myself. The scene unwound in slow motion. I leveled the gun at her head and cocked the hammer. "You don't understand! It doesn't matter how much we sell! We are so far in debt that the bank is about to take this place and everything on it!"

She screamed again, but it did no good. I heard the click as I pulled the trigger, and it was done. Reality set in as I watched her body go limp, blood flowing freely from the gaping wound in beautiful Matilda's head. I dropped to my knees and raised my hands to heaven, crying out as loudly as humanly possible. "What have I done?"

Now, there was no other option. Matilda was gone. The farm was gone. I had nothing left. I knew someone was bound to find us. I knew there would need to be an explanation. I reached into my pocket, withdrew a pad of paper and a pencil, and wrote a quick note.

*To whoever finds this:*
*I'm sorry for what I have done.*
*I could no longer take care of my family.*
*I need it to end.*
*This is the only way I know how.*
*Now, the property can be someone else's dream without me losing it,*
*-Cecil Amos*

The gun was in my left hand. In my other hand was the newly penned note. I placed the paper in the front pocket of my overalls, where it was still partially visible. Then, I placed the muzzle of the revolver into my own mouth and pulled the trigger.

The world went black...Then, light again...I was...floating... I could see our bodies. Beside me, looking down at them was Matilda. I shook my head. How could we both be bodies on the ground, yet be *looking* at our bodies on the ground? I soon realized, looking at Matilda, that she was almost transparent, and she was floating, too. We had left our physical bodies... We were... ghosts.

Matilda looked forlorn as she stared down at her own body. Then she raised her transparent hands as if to examine them. "Cecil, what have you done to us?" She moaned.

A sudden pang of regret struck me. I tried to move towards her, but she drifted away at a pace not possible for a human.

"Cecil, had you just let me speak, I would have told you." She grasped her abdomen. "Despite your abuse, the last time you forced yourself on me, a child was conceived. I was pregnant. Now you have killed us both!"

I could not believe what I was hearing. We had tried so hard for so long to conceive another offspring, and finally, we had given up. Then, when things were at their worst, something magical had happened. I had ruined it. I had ruined it all! I could no longer look at her nor face what I had done.

I took off towards the edge of the property. As I met the edge, it was as if I was struck by lightning. I fell back and closed my eyes. When I opened them, I discovered that I was back at the site where I had died. I tried several more times with the same result. I could see Matilda watching quietly. I finally deduced that we could not leave this place, though I did not know why. I was stuck with the woman whom I had once loved and then loathed and finally murdered with my own hands. What ironic punishment. I realized I had gotten my wish. If I were to be trapped, at least it was in the place that I desired to stay.

I watched with dread as Harold drove to the yard to do the chores that day after our deaths. I had hoped that he would not be the one to find us. He had been a loyal friend and did not deserve the sight that lay before him. He appeared stunned as he reached the gory scene. He shook his head slowly as he spoke to my lifeless body. Though he could not read, I suspected he knew what was written in the note. He stood staring between Matilda's body, still hanging chained to the tree, and my body not far away on the ground, still holding the gun.

"One more favor, boss..."

I watched the gentle giant carefully heft my body over his shoulder and position it in our home. Next, he carefully unlocked Matilda's body from the tree, never allowing her to touch the ground, and positioned her body in front of mine. He kicked dirt over the pools of blood in the areas where we had died, doing his best to hide the scene of the crime. He made a mess of the house so that it appeared that a robbery had been committed, and I had died attempting to protect my wife. He took a lockbox from inside the house and placed the note and the gun in it. He buried it in the barn near the hydrant. To my dismay, he had completely forgotten the lock and chain hanging from the tree. I hoped I had hidden it well enough that his illusion would be believable.

He completed the chores in silence and then drove off. When he returned, the sheriff was with him. I heard him struggle to explain what had happened, forcing the words out as clearly as he could.

The Sheriff was able to piece together murder and robbery from Harold's garbled speech. They briefly investigated, concluded that Harold was correct, and then left.

Time passed slowly after our death. When you are dead, you have no concept of minutes and hours passing. It all begins to blur together. Matilda tried to speak to me several times. I could not bear the shame. I treated her cruelly, hoping she would stop and leave me alone. Eventually, she did. I was alone, unable to communicate with anyone. I was left to deal with the consequences of my actions. A curse worse than anything I could have imagined. I became more and more bitter.

# Part 22: Life as ... GHOSTS

Part 22: Life as ... GHOSTS

The remainder of the farm was auctioned off shortly after our deaths had been declared a murder, committed presumably by a desperate drifter. The authorities had determined that we had no living heirs, and the bank owned the property anyway.

Everything we had left was taken and sold. The animals, gaunt and barely breathing, were auctioned off for almost nothing. The money went straight back to the bank, itself collapsing, yet still capable of collecting its due.

I yelled, screamed, and flailed my arms, yet no one could see or hear me aside from Matilda. She seemed to have resigned to being stuck on the farm in this lonely existence. I had not. I was just as stubborn in death as I had been in life and twice as mean. I committed myself to attempting to manipulate people and the things around me until I was somehow able to let the living know that I was still here. If I had to be stuck here, I was going to make sure that whoever came to own this cursed piece of land would suffer a similar fate.

Each day, I became stronger as I practiced. Finally, I did it—the first couple who bought what was left of the farm after our death met a terrible fate. As the young man leaned over the cistern looking for water, I gave him a shove from behind. He fell head-first into the cistern with his head bouncing against the cement sides several times on the way down. He landed face down in the shallow water on the bottom and never woke up. His wife was left a broken woman and moved back home to her parents, leaving the farm vacant yet again. Without payment, the farm once again reverted to the bank.

The depression was still in full effect. After our death and yet another death, word was beginning to spread that there was something strange about 13 Mile Farm. As money was short, and there was no tillable land left, only the house, outbuildings, and fruit trees, the farm was not highly sought after. The grass grew long despite the lack of water and the ever-present dust. The land sat empty, and once again, I had no company aside from Matilda.

I continued to ignore her and practice my newly found gift. I learned more tricks as I worked on my skills. I was as brilliant in death as I had been in life. Matilda, however, did nothing with her time. She seemed to have no skills in the afterlife and no desire to develop any. This continued for several more years until 1939, when the depression finally ended.

I noticed the subtle differences. First, the air cleared. Then, as it did, the grass grew in short, luscious clumps. Even a few of the flowers in Matilda's neglected flower beds came back. For the first time since we had passed away, the fruit trees bore flowers instead of only leaves. Though overgrown, the place began to show a glimpse of its former beauty. Matilda appeared happier at seeing this, as I observed her from afar.

Yet again, another young couple made their home on *our* farm, disturbing my peace. This time, they had a baby. This stirred emotions in me that I had forgotten existed. I looked at Matilda and remembered her words to me after we had died. We had finally conceived again, though it was done in anger, and now that baby would never have a life, thanks to me. I was jealous, angry, and more ashamed than I had ever been. I knew I could not harm this lovely young woman and her baby, but her husband...

Fate intervened for me. Our nation had gone to war. Something called "The Draft" was implemented in 1940. As it turned out, the young husband was a middle son, over twenty-one, and in good health—the perfect candidate to fight for his country. Not long after, he was sent away to be trained and then go to war. The brave young woman vowed to stay at their home and take care of everything while he was gone. Four more years dragged by. The baby grew. Though lonely, the young woman survived. I did not bother her. I was happy to watch. The letters from the young husband lessened and then stopped. The young woman became very concerned.

On a Saturday in 1945, almost exactly five years after the couple had moved to the farm, a military truck clattered up the driveway to the farmhouse. Inside were two men dressed in green military uniforms. The young woman, who had been tending to her garden, slowly straightened. She gathered her son in her arms, suspecting what she feared had come true. She hugged her son tightly as the men approached.

"Mrs. Brown? Mrs. Anthony Brown?" One of the men addressed her.

"Yes." She said in a shaky voice.

"I'm sorry. Your husband has been killed in action." The man handed her an envelope.

"Thank you," she whispered, her eyes welled with tears.

The Officer saluted, and both soldiers climbed back into the waiting vehicle. Only then did she allow herself to cry.

Mrs. Brown had kept her promise to her husband. She had waited. Now, he was gone. She determined that the place they had made a home would forever remind her of him. She could not stay. Matilda and I watched sadly as she packed their belongings and left the farm without looking back.

The years went on, and I continued to try to escape. Each attempt was futile. It was as if an invisible wall bordered the property. I grew angrier and more bored each year. With my only entertainment being the torture of each new resident of my farm, I came up with new, increasingly worse ways to force their departure. I ensured that no new resident could stay longer than five years, which was the length of time Matilda and I had been alive on the farm. I discovered that I was most powerful when the living residents of 13 Mile Farm tried to make improvements. I did not like seeing changes to what I had built with my own two hands. When this activity started, I went on a rampage.

The tragedies grew worse as my anger festered. With each generation that passed, the plots I came up with became more diabolical. I was the cause of divorces, injuries, sickness, and even death. All this caused these hopeful new faces to leave within five years, like Matilda and I had been forced to.

Matilda continued begging and trying to persuade me to stop, but her pleas met deaf ears. I could see her trying to warn the farm residents, but she was not strong enough. I met her attempts with fits of rage. I could no longer harm her physically, but I could still scream at her, causing her further heartache. For some reason, she still held out hope that, in death, I would return to being her once-beloved husband.

# Part 23: Cecil Meets His Match

Part 23: Cecil Meets His Match

In the mid-2000s, the last couple I was ever to challenge moved to my farm. I sensed them as they drove up to the farm to look at it for the first time late at night. There was something different about that young lady. She reminded me of... Matilda. Their looks were remarkably the same. This young woman, however, seemed much feistier. I could sense her spunk as soon as they neared the farm. I knew I was going to have to work hard to dissuade this young woman from staying here.

By this time, the farm was in very poor condition. It had been through so many owners that it was practically being given away. I had caused enough fighting between the last couple that they had divorced. The farm had been given to them by her father after his wife had become afflicted with Cancer.

To my dismay, I could not reach the young couple as they were outside the property's borders. I hoped my sense of the young woman was correct, and that she saw what the farm used to be when she looked at it. I closed my eyes and concentrated as hard as I could. I pressed my fingers to my temples, trying to send my thoughts telepathically to whichever one of them was open. *You are drawn to this place. You want to come back and look at it when it is light. You see the potential and want to make this place your home.*

When I opened my eyes, the car moved past the farm and turned around. They slowed as they passed it again. Now, all I could do was wait to see if the seed had been planted.

To my delight, they returned. This time with a chatty realtor. Now, it was he that I attempted to persuade. I spoke silently to him, making sure that he spoke only good words about the farm, and did so convincingly. I followed along as he took them through the house. I stood in the hallway as they entered the second level of the house. The young woman stopped and stared for a moment, looking directly at me. I thought briefly that she could see me. She muttered to herself, shook her head as if trying to wake up, and continued the tour with the young man and the relator.

I could see that they were going to the barn next. Anger flashed within me. I hated the thought of anyone entering the barn. It was a sacred space to me. It was where we were married. The player piano from Matilda's parents still stood in the loft. I could not prevent them from entering; however, I could dissuade them from wanting to be there. I made my way to the barn and seated myself on the top of the piano, listening patiently as they roamed the rest of the building.

I could feel her energy before I saw her. I heard her coming up the stairs. An idea formed itself in my head. With my strength growing, and the young woman seemingly receptive, could I possibly make myself visible to her? I closed my eyes again, putting forth so much effort that it hurt. I saw her look at her arms. I could see the hair rising and goosebumps appearing. I saw her place her hand over her mouth as if she were about to be sick. I was thrilled! It was working. I forced myself to strain harder. Breaking my concentration, the moose of a man she was with clomped his way up the stairs, followed by the jabbering realtor. The connection was broken as he urged her to move aside so that he could see the loft. Buffoon... I will deal with you later...

He picked up a long-forgotten basketball that had been left behind by one of the many residents I had previously driven away and lofted it towards the rusty, crooked hoop on the barn wall. I snickered as he missed his mark by a landslide. For fun, I slid off the piano and hit a key with one finger. She seemed to hear it, though no one else did, and questioned the others. They confirmed that they had heard nothing. I smiled. I was reaching her. I hit several more keys. She froze. I knew she could see the keys moving and hear the notes coming from the old player's piano. She looked ill.

Her attention was drawn away by the buffoon jumping up and down on the hayloft floor as if to prove a point. I rolled my eyes. If I could convince them to move here, these two would be my best accomplishments to date.

Then she looked my way again. This time, I was sure she saw me standing there right in front of the buffoon. I willed her to see me, not him. She was looking at him as if she did not know him. I scowled at her and tried with all my might to will her out of my space. She began to cough and then fell backward into a pile of decaying straw.

The realtor and the buffoon rushed to aid her. They quickly helped her to her feet and questioned what had happened. She seemed unsure of what had happened herself and quickly made an excuse. They exited the loft and quickly went back outside. I realized I had achieved my goal.

I watched from a distance as they examined each aspect of the property that the realtor pointed out. I became a bit concerned when they neared the remainder of the orchard. There, behind the tree, was Matilda. The realtor relayed the story of the fruit grove or what he knew of it. I smiled as I recalled the day that I had secretly had the trees planted as a wedding present for Matilda. I looked over at her behind her favorite pear tree. A pang of regret shot through me, leaving me momentarily paralyzed.

The young woman squinted towards the pear tree and cocked her head. Matilda, who had been hiding behind the tree, had poked her head out to get a closer look at the young woman. I watched the young woman rub her eyes as if trying to clear them of unwanted debris. I then reacted quickly. "Matilda! Don't!" I yelled, pushing her back behind the tree. Could this young woman see Matilda as well?

Part 24: Can I Make Them Leave

To my elation, the young couple purchased the farm. I observed quietly as they, along with friends and family, moved their possessions into the house. They all happily chattered amongst themselves as I floated above them, watching and listening. Their chatter had already included a discussion of improvements the young couple wanted to make to the property. I smirked and pressed my fingers together in a steeple formation as I considered what I could do to thwart their efforts.

Matilda was keeping her distance. We had 10 acres we could inhabit, making it easy to avoid each other when we wanted to. I found it strange, as she usually tried to intervene in my mischief as soon as I started, sometimes spoiling my fun. I wondered if she was up to something. After the young woman appeared to see her, she kept her distance.

I allowed them to move things in, doing nothing other than observing. On the day they started painting, I decided to begin small. The young lady seemed on edge. She always seemed to be looking over her shoulder or around her. I knew she could sense that we were here. I was carefully biding my time and building strength before showing myself again.

The young lady and another, who seemed to be close, had entered the house with cans of what I guessed was paint, some plastic, and other assorted supplies. They chatted easily amongst themselves as they worked together, removing pictures and decorations from the walls and placing furniture in the center of the room. After they had finished placing the plastic to protect the floor, I watched the one who did not live in the house pick up a can and dance around shaking it. The woman who did belong raised an eyebrow at her, groaning at her friend's silliness. The little dark-haired woman did not mind.

The two of them got more serious as they looked at the large task that was before them. The dark-haired one picked up her phone and called someone. The ladies started painting the living room walls a light tan color. Soon afterward, a man I had not seen before arrived and began to help, as well. The buffoon was not usually present in the evenings, so I assumed that this new man was there to provide muscle in his absence.

The time was right. I floated over to the ladder where the paint can sat and swatted at it with all my might. At first, it only moved slightly. The group did not notice. I backed up, this time putting forth all the energy I could muster, and ran at the can perched precariously on the platform portion of the ladder. The can teetered briefly, then clattered to the floor. Paint poured from the wide mouth of the opening and splashed onto the coffee table sitting next to it.

The group froze. The man was first to speak. "What was that?" The two women appeared too startled to speak. I had achieved my goal! Unfortunately, fear did not seem to stop the determined young woman. She had made up her mind to make my home into her own. I would have to try harder next time.

Several weeks passed before anything of note changed. The room had been successfully painted, despite my attempted intervention. I felt drained, and knew moving something was a task that I could not often attempt due to the energy it took. The young couple made no further changes for a bit. The next change was not to the house. It was the arrival of animals. While lounging on the piano in the barn, I heard horses whinnying and pawing as a pickup pulled a trailer into the driveway. This was an unexpected turn of events. The barn had not housed animals in many years! I was not sure how I felt about life inhabiting its walls once again.

The young lady ran towards the trailer with excitement. An older man unfolded his tall, lean frame from the driver's side of the truck and hugged the young lady. They had a brief discussion. Meanwhile, I was near the trailer, speaking quietly to the black horse. She pawed nervously, reared, and whinnied as I spoke. The second brown horse seemed curious, but not spooked by my presence. He seemed to watch me curiously, but had no reaction.

The young lady cautiously opened the trailer's doors. It was clear this was her horse. She spoke to the animal gently, attempting to calm the wild-eyed animal and coax her out of the trailer. I knew the animal was aware of my presence. This could be my chance. *Could I coerce the horse into injuring her owner?*

As the horse backed out of the trailer, I charged towards her, hands flailing and yelling as loud as I could. The horse snorted and then let out a shrill cry filled with fear. She reared high on her hind legs, pawing at the sky, catching the young lady off guard and knocking her backward. The lead rope flew from her hand, and she fell hard onto her back, hitting her head and knocking the wind out of her. I curled my lips into a smug smile. As she tried to stand, she looked directly at me. Again, it was as if she had briefly seen me.

The young man and the older man, presumably her father were by her side almost immediately, discouraging further reaction. She quickly recovered, scowling at the men's attempt to help her. She grabbed the lead rope and, taking a deep breath, attempted to calm herself and the horse. The action was over. To my delight, I had once again been seen, although the intended damage was not done. The fun for the evening was over, and I felt weak after exercising my growing powers.

I was quiet for some time following the incident with the horse. My attempts to terrify the young lady into leaving the farm had, so far, been unsuccessful. This was going to take some careful thought, and more than likely all of the power I could muster. Next, I would attempt to influence the young man. I stroked my chin as I sat on the piano in the loft, trying to formulate a plan.

I began with something simple: I started appearing in his dreams. It affected his sleep and made him constantly surly. The young couple clearly loved each other, as I had never seen them fight. The similarities to Matilda and I's previous happiness were too much for me to bear. They were upsetting me more each day. They wanted to hold their wedding in the loft, as Matilda and I had. They had even started clearing the straw out. I noticed that the young man wore a ring on a chain around his neck. It appeared to be old and a treasured object to both. I wondered what would happen if it disappeared. Was I capable of removing an object from his body without him noticing? The idea became increasingly enticing as I contemplated it.

As I watched them toiling away, hot and exhausted, I hypothesized that if something went awry now, it might be just enough to instigate a fight. I levitated directly above the large man, now bent over with a pitchfork in hand, gathering a load of the dusty straw. The young woman was faced the opposite way, so if I were careful enough, the only person who would notice would be the man. I carefully extended my arm and a finger down to the loose chain. As I touched it, the man swatted at the area I touched and stood back up.

"Must have been a fly," he mumbled.

Drat! My attempt had been detected. I hovered above him a bit longer, contemplating what other method might work. All at once, it came to me. The clasp! Why not simply undo the clasp and allow gravity to take its course with the piece of jewelry? Again, I floated over him. This time, I leaned over his back, careful not to touch him. Manipulating something as small as the clasp was much more complicated than manipulating anything I had previously. It took what seemed like hours. Eventually, I was able to unhook it, and I watched the silver chain drop to the floor, undetected by the large young man.

After some time, the couple had scooped the last bit of straw out of the loft door. The man had yet to notice his missing jewelry. I watched it slip into a crack in the floorboards, which would be nearly impossible to find. Shortly after my achievement, it seemed that the couple had finished their task and were quitting for the day. They dropped their tools, and I followed as they walked toward the house. Now, all I had to do was watch and wait. I hoped the desired reaction would be reached.

The man went upstairs to the bathroom. The young woman began to prepare a meal in the kitchen. I floated above her, looking on in disgust. I could not stand seeing her look out the window the same way Matilda always had. It was not long before the man came back downstairs without his shirt. His posture said all I needed to know. His head hung, and he grasped at his neckline where the chain had previously hung.

It was as if I were watching the fuse to a powder keg burn slowly toward igniting the powder within. I watched her face change from happy to furious. I watched her stance change as she planted her feet and balled her hands into fists. Then the screaming started. He bent to her whim, succumbing to her fury, and the two spent the rest of the evening sorting through the straw in hopes of finding the ring. I laughed as I realized they were looking in the wrong place!

The ring and chain were to remain forever lost in the crack between the loft floorboards. She retreated in her car, leaving an angry cloud of dust and did not return that evening.

Had I succeeded in driving her away? Would this force them off my land and stop the changes from being made?

# Part 25: A Wedding Too Similar

Part 25: A Wedding Too Similar

I had failed yet again. The young woman returned, and they appeared happily in love again. I began to catch glimpses of Matilda. She kept her distance; however, I began to see her near the young woman more frequently. She smiled as she listened to the young lovers make the final plans for their wedding. I became more agitated by the day. What was I doing wrong? How had my attempts not yet been enough to scare them away? Indeed, these were a different type of people.

The day of the wedding came. There appeared to be no way to prevent it. I watched from near the cleaned-up piano, arms crossed and utterly distraught. This happy scene was all too familiar! Matilda, too, was present. She stood across the loft from me, watching me as much as she was watching the couple, the guests, and the wedding party.

Finally, it was over. It was time for the newly married couple to make their way back up to the loft. Time for me to be a nuisance! I jumped towards the large young man as the photographer snapped a picture. For a moment, I felt he and I merge into one, but then I slipped to the other side of him. I wondered if I had possessed him, if only for a second. Could I be capable of such an immense task? The big oaf did not seem to notice, though the young woman appeared to have a strange look on her face. Matilda watched in horror, knowing what I had just done.

The couple moved to the center of the floor, and a spotlight shone on them. Now, it was my turn to watch in horror. Matilda slowly floated towards the young woman. Gently, she placed her hands on the young woman's shoulders and then disappeared. There was no change to the young woman's movements as she danced with her new husband, but there was a definite change in her eyes. Her eyes became Matilda's. I immediately knew that Matilda had been watching and learning. She had possessed the young woman and must have been doing so for a while now.

Matilda returned after a few tense moments, looking exhausted yet pleased with herself. The young woman leaned in closer to her new husband, fear in her eyes. What had Matilda done? I was tired from my activity, so I didn't dare try to find the answer at the time.

After their wedding, time moved on, and the couple continued to make improvements. It slowly changed into a place I barely recognized. The time table I had set for myself to remove them was ticking closer to being up. In the history of being a ghost, I had yet failed to remove a family from my land within five years. It was a trend I did not intend to break. This couple, too, must go!

I continued to torment the young man in his sleep. I watched his personality change noticeably. He seemed to go from a doting husband to almost... resentful. When she asked him for help, he grew increasingly irritable. He would complete whatever task was asked of him, clearly very unhappy about doing so. Between the exhaustion and the stress, he began to consume large amounts of alcohol. The young woman noticed and tolerated it, even after I had persuaded him to damage her precious car.

Once again, I needed to thwart Matilda's attempt to divulge our secret to the young woman. I caught her as the young woman sat under that damn pear tree, crying. Matilda had made herself visible! She had even been able to touch the young woman's shoulder! She had shown herself to the woman exactly as she had been before I had killed her, bruised and crying! She had opened her mouth and tried to speak, but I pulled her away before she could, causing us both to disappear. As she faded, she pointed a finger towards the tree where we had died. Drat! I hoped she had not noticed.

Matilda was furious with me after that. She screamed at me with so much might that her form faded in and out. She flailed her arms and told me she would do everything within her power to save this couple who were so much like us. I laughed in her face as I watched her weaken more and more until her form disappeared.

The young woman was shaken. I could see that she wanted to tell someone, but I could not stop her. She got in her car and sped out of the driveway. I could not believe her dedication. It was clear that she took her commitment to her husband more seriously than anything else. She was so very much like my Matilda.

By then, it no longer felt like a choice. I shaped her husband the same way I myself had been shaped, slowly and without force, until it felt natural to him. No one ever noticed—how could they? I came to him in his sleep, never the same face, never the same place, only the same familiar weight settling into his thoughts. I spoke of long hours and thankless work, of a life spent bending for others until there was nothing left. I told him what I once told myself—that a man can only endure so much before something in him hardens. That learning to say no was strength. That anger was earned. Each night he woke a little more convinced, a little more distant, carrying thoughts he believed were his own. The end of his marriage would not come suddenly. It would come the way mine had—quietly, inevitably. I did not question it. This was simply how it went. This was what men like us became.

# Part 26: Celeste Gets Involved

Part 26: Celeste Gets Involved

The young wife seemed to be getting wise to me. I had heard her speak to her pesky best friend, relating that something strange was going on. I observed that friend on multiple occasions during her visits. I had a feeling that she could sense me, as well. Several times, I could have sworn she looked straight at me. It was very strange to me as I had made no attempt to communicate with her or make myself known. Was it possible that she had a sixth sense?

When the young wife left after her car was damaged, I had also heard her tell her husband that she was going to visit her best friend. I was sure she was up to something. The young woman returned several hours later, seemingly calmer. There was a discussion between her and her husband about a large party and a bonfire at the farm with all their friends.

I watched, unable to do anything, as the party happened around me. As a ghost, I quickly found that if I used too much energy, I was unable to do anything for quite some time afterward. The frustration was nearly unbearable.

It only got worse from there. The people at the party seemed completely oblivious as the young woman and her best friend snuck away. I could hear them giggling and plotting to destroy my piano. I could not let that happen. They would push my beloved piano out the loft door and burn it! My strength had not returned yet. I felt helpless. I couldn't even muster enough strength to move an object, let alone do anything to draw attention to myself. I even tried to draw the buffoon husband's attention.

Nothing worked. I watched in dismay as the two young women pushed the piano towards the door. It teetered on the edge for a moment, giving me a glimmer of hope that they were not strong enough to complete the task. The stubborn best friend refused to be beaten by what she saw as a simple piece of furniture. She gave it one final shove. The piano lurched forward and fell to the ground, making an awful sound. It splintered into pieces, and as if it were crying, a final bally of notes sounded as the instrument met its fate. I cried out as loud as I could. No one to hear me other than Matilda. She stood expressionless on the other end of the barn as if she did not care.

The rage I felt fueled my strength. I was unable to do anything about the piano's destruction, but I could make the young woman's life miserable after it had happened. I would get to that large buffoon of a husband as soon as I was able and make *him* get my retribution. I swore vengeance on her best friend, who was helping the young wife. All of them would pay dearly!

By that night, I had regained some strength. I allowed the woman to sleep in peace. It seemed any attempt to affect her was futile. Instead, I mustered all the strength I had and jumped inside the young husband's body. I tormented him throughout the night.

The next day, the young woman had been busy cleaning up, making breakfast, and seeing her friends off. I had paid her no attention. I had seen her come inside and lie down on the couch. It seemed she was feeling a bit ill. She was weakened. Perfect timing.

"Wake up.... Waaaaake uppppp..." I screamed in the young man's head. I was still in his body. I was in control as he opened his eyes. They changed to my eyes as he blinked. I directed him down the stairs and out the door to where the remainder of the piano lay amongst the ashes. I willed him to pick up a key and the scroll where the music had once been housed. He did not even fight me. It seemed as if he were still asleep. Next, I directed him to his sleeping wife on the couch. His body stood over her, and I spoke through him.

"What did you do to my piano?" I growled through gritted teeth. As she awoke to him standing angrily over her, for the first time, she seemed scared and confused. I threw down the pieces of the piano and raised his hands to strangle her. "That piano was a wedding gift to us! How can it mean so little to you?"

She ducked to avoid my grasp, making herself small as she curled into a ball on the corner of the couch. The couple's newly acquired puppy charged at me as I attempted to grab his owner and harm her like I had wanted to do for so long. I kicked the puppy, a bare foot connecting with its ribs, and sent it flying. It yelped in pain, which pulled the young woman out of her fearful state. She scooped up the puppy and backpedaled toward the door.

At that very moment, realizing what he had almost allowed me to do, the man fought for control back. I was expelled from his body and flew backward so powerfully that I flew through the back wall of the house. The buffoon had somehow managed to overpower me! How could this be? Had I not allowed enough time to regain my strength? Now, there would be further suspicion!

I needed to think. What else could I possibly do? The young woman left again that evening, but I knew that was more of a negative than a positive, as I was sure she was bound for her best friend's house to try to form another plan. All their plotting had only served to further anger me. I just needed to regain enough strength to do something worse. I muttered a loud curse, not knowing if it would be effective, knowing it would doom her best friend to poor health if she assisted the young woman any further. Was I too weak?

# Part 27: No Further Help Required

Part 27: No Further Help Required

As it turned out, nothing further than what I had already done was required. I was able to sit back and watch as their marriage crumbled. His drinking got worse. She became more and more withdrawn. I could feel her sadness and, along with it, Matilda's. I was winning! I had caused the broken hydrant in the barn. I had watched with joy as he had thrown a drunken fit when her parents had come to help repair it in his absence.

Now, I felt the end coming near. She had received a phone call and left in a hurry. I had a feeling it was him. I wished with all my being that I could follow her into town to see what had happened.

They returned home, but she did not stay. She turned around and left him standing helplessly in the driveway as she threw rocks with the back tires of the truck in a dramatic exit. I laughed in excitement. She couldn't possibly have any desire to return to him, as angry as she was. I didn't know what he had done, but by her reaction, it was something awful.

I was wrong! She did return. The painful relationship seemed to be hanging on by a thread, but they had yet to give up. As I say this, I believe she was the only one holding on. He appeared to have given up on everything. He did absolutely nothing. He never left the house. Even I became disappointed in him. I had never tolerated laziness well. I had hoped that their relationship would end, but not like this. I stopped interfering; determining that nothing more was needed.

After a bad blizzard, she returned home. She had paperwork with her. She wanted a divorce. Then he was there alone. For some reason, he stayed. Like me, he knew he could not pay the bills but stayed, trying to find a way. I was surprised to see this much action from a man who had seemed dormant for so long. Despite his best efforts, he lost the farm. I watched as the police came and escorted him, kicking and fighting, from the property in a squad car. This was it. The moment I had been waiting for, but somehow, I didn't feel any sense of accomplishment. Instead, I felt the same sense of despair I had right before I had killed Matilda and then myself.

I had gotten what I wanted, yet the victory felt empty this time. Again, the farm sat empty. I was alone with Matilda. What I didn't know was that Matilda had spoken to the young lady before she left.

I could hear explosions and see the bright bursts of color in the sky. I was bored, so I sat on a stump and watched. To my surprise, a familiar vehicle pulled into the driveway, and then another. It was the young lady, her friends, and her family. I stood up and floated closer to catch their conversation. They were there to celebrate one final holiday on the farm that the young lady had loved so much. Matilda floated nearby, smiling. I could feel the sadness exuding from the young woman. I could not figure out why Matilda seemed happy.

I dismissed it and stayed near the group as they shot their fireworks. Then, the young lady and her best friend disappeared into the house. Both reappeared with puffy red eyes as if they had been crying. They rejoined a young man whom I was unfamiliar with near the tree grove.

I looked more carefully. They were standing near the tree where we had died. They were looking directly at the now rusty lock! The unfamiliar young man cocked the hammer of a pistol and aimed directly at the lock. I did not know what was happening, but I suddenly began to feel ill. This was a feeling that I had not experienced since I was living. I hovered nearby, trying to relieve the pain in my stomach, no longer paying any attention to the group near the tree. He shot and missed again. The stabbing pain in my abdomen became worse. The young man paused, took a deep breath, focused on his aim, and slowly exhaled. This time, he hit his mark.

I screamed in anguish! The lock that had caused Matilda so much pain shattered as his bullet hit. Bright light burst from what was left of the lock, and night became day. Now, Matilda was by my side. No longer did she appear battered and thin. She appeared as the same young woman I had met and fallen in love with long ago. Abruptly, the sky opened. Matilda smiled down at us as she drifted upwards in a beam of blinding light. "I forgive you." She uttered as she turned her face skyward and ascended until she was out of sight.

I tried to reach for her, discovering that fiery chains had formed around my body, binding my arms to my torso and leaving my body burning where they had touched. The ground cracked and then opened, revealing a fiery bottomless pit below.

I began to feel myself being sucked downward by an unseen force at the other end of the chains that were binding me. I tried to claw at the earth to save myself; however, my attempts were futile. I looked up at the crowd as I slowly descended into what I could only imagine was hell. My screams for mercy went unheard. And that's how I ended up here. Now you have heard the story of my life.

The man had sat through my entire story paying close attention, without a word. As I concluded, he shifted in his seat. "Cecil, I am not who you think." His appearance changed as he spoke. No longer was his appearance that of the other prisoners in this Circle of Hell, tattered, dirty, and faceless. The burnt appearance of his skin changed to an alabaster white. His eyes went from dark black holes to glowing blue. He grew to almost the height of the ceiling. His hair was long, falling to his shoulders in golden locks. The tattered rags he had once worn became a long, flowing robe tied at his midsection with a braided golden rope. On his once bare feet were leather sandals. The smile upon his face seemed sincere. I stared back in awe.

"I am Haniel, God's angel of grace. I was sent here to hear your story and determine whether you are to remain here or if you are worthy of a second chance. You have given me much to think about, especially hearing everything that has led you to being placed here. I do not believe that you are entirely bad..."

# Author Biography

Christina Lynne writes from the heart of South Dakota, where small-town life often finds its way into her stories.

Christina Lynne, creates heartfelt, faith-based fiction that speaks to readers of all ages—stories about loss, love, faith, and finding one's way back to hope.

Her debut novella, *13 Miles North*, is a love-lost story with a twist—born out of personal experience and the healing that comes through faith and writing. Its companion, *Cecil's Story*, gives voice to the so-called villain, reminding readers that every story has more than one side. Her children's book, *The Rusty Kitten*, shares a simple but powerful truth with young readers: that it's perfectly all right to be exactly who God made you to be.

Christina has been a storyteller since her school days, when a beloved teacher first encouraged her to publish her work. Life, however, had other plans. She spent years working in the business and financial world before rediscovering her calling as a writer—a rediscovery sparked by grief, friendship, and faith. Through loss and new beginnings, Christina learned that even broken chapters can become part of something beautiful.

Every book she writes carries a piece of her journey—her experiences, her faith, and her belief that stories can heal. She hopes her readers, young and old alike, find comfort and inspiration in her words and the reminder that it's never too late to follow your purpose.

When she's not writing, Christina enjoys quiet moments with her husband, time with her family, and connecting with other authors through her group, *Author Advice and Insights*. You can follow her writing journey on Facebook and Instagram at **Christina Lynne Writes** or reach her directly at christinalynnewrites@gmail.com

# Reader's Reviews

"Engaging, gripping, heartfelt, and supernatural elements all rolled into one. This story is a page-turner that will keep you guessing until the very end. The crescendo is well worth the wait!"

Kimberley Hall Author: *A Journey of A Thousand Miles.*

"Christina's passion for her craft shines through in her writing. I deeply admire her work ethic, creativity, and relentless pursuit of excellence. Each of her books leaves a lasting impact, resonating long after the final page is turned."

M. Keil Hackley Author: *Undercurrent: A woman's story of breaking free & the horse who saves her*

.

# Other Books By the Author

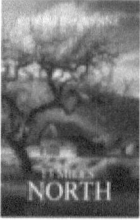